THE TOWN THAT I'd grown up in and had always called Dullsville was no longer dull. Not only was I dating a vampire, but now two other teen Nosferatus were living among Dullsvillians, whose biggest concern was getting the best price on the newest Prada purses or the latest Big Bertha golf clubs.

I was the only mortal who knew about the secret identity of the new bloodsucking inhabitants and I was dying to spill my guts to the *Dullsville Dispatch*. The front-page headline would read: GOTH GIRL GETS THE GOODS! Raven Madison Wins Nobel Peace Prize for Unearthing the Undead. Below, a color photograph would feature me standing next to Luna, Jagger, and Alexander—and I'd be the only one reflected in the picture.

But in lieu of blabbing my discoveries to the world, I would have to keep Jagger's and Luna's ghastly secret to myself—that the twins were really vampires.

PRAISE FOR
Vampire Kisses

An ALA Quick Pick for Young Adult Readers
A New York Public Library Book for the Teen Age

"All in all, a good read for those who want a vampire love story without the gore." —*School Library Journal*

"As in her *Teenage Mermaid*, Schreiber adds some refreshing twists to genre archetypes and modern-day stereotypes." —*Publishers Weekly*

"Horror hooks such as a haunted mansion, a romantic teenage vampire, and a dark heroine who wins against the golden guys make this a title that readers will bite into with Goth gusto."
—*The Bulletin of the Center for Children's Books*

"Schreiber uses a careful balance of humor, irony, pathos, and romance as she develops a plot that introduces the possibility of a real vampire."—ALA *Booklist*

Ellen Schreiber

Vampire Kisses 3

—◆—

Vampireville

KATHERINE TEGEN BOOKS
HARPERTEEN
An Imprint of HarperCollins*Publishers*

HarperTeen is an imprint of HarperCollins Publishers.

Vampire Kisses 3: Vampireville
Copyright © 2006 by Ellen Schreiber
Library of Congress Cataloging-in-Publication Data
Schreiber, Ellen.
    Vampire kisses 3 : Vampireville / Ellen Schreiber.— 1st ed.
       p.   cm.
    Summary: As teen vampire twins Luna and Jagger try to trick a high
school soccer star into bonding with Luna for eternity, sixteen-year-old
goth girl Raven Madison and her vampire boyfriend, Alexander, strive
to save him.
    ISBN 978-0-06-077627-5
    [1. Vampires—Fiction.] I. Title: Vampire kisses three. II. Title:
Vampireville. III. Title.
PZ7.53787Vamc 2006   2005022863
[Fic]—dc22   CIP
                                                                 AC

❖

First HarperTeen paperback edition, 2007

To my parents,
Gary and Suzanne Schreiber,
with love and vampire kisses

CONTENTS

"I'm looking for someone to quench my thirst—
for all eternity."
—Luna Maxwell

I was ready to become a vampire.

I stood alone in the middle of Dullsville's cemetery, dressed in a black corset minidress, fishnet stockings, and my signature combat boots. I held a small bouquet of dead black roses in my black fingerless gloves. A vintage midnight-colored lace veil dripped down over my pale face, gracefully shrouding my black lipstick and eye shadow.

My vampire to be, Alexander Sterling, wearing a gray pallbearer's suit and hat, waited a few yards ahead of me by our gothic altar—a closed coffin adorned with a candelabra and a pewter goblet.

The scene was breathtaking. Fog floated through the graveyard like wayward ghosts. Candles flickered atop tombstones and were scattered alongside graves. A group of bats hovered over a cluster of lonely trees. Raindrops began to fall as the faint sound of screeching violins and a discordant harpsichord sent icy chills through my veins.

I had waited an eternity for this moment. My childhood fantasy was now coming true—I would be a dark angel of the night. I was as excited as a groupie who was about to marry a rock star.

Tiny torches lit my path, like a gothic runway. But as I took my first step toward Alexander, I began to wonder if I was making the right choice. My heart started to race as I proceeded forward. Images of the life I would be leaving behind flashed before me. My mom helping me sew a black velvet tote for my home ec. project. I took a step. Watching *Dracula* on DVD with my dad. Another step. Even my nerdy brother, Billy Boy, kindly helping me with my math homework.

Step. My best friend, Becky, and I trying to climb the Mansion's gate. Step. My new kitty, Nightmare, gently purring in my arms. Step. They all began to haunt me.

In one bite my life would change forever.

I was leaving a boring, safe, yet love-filled world of the living and committing an eternity to a dangerous, unknown, darkened world of the undead.

As I continued to walk down the cemetery aisle, I could see the back of Alexander who, now only a few feet away, lifted a goblet from the coffin.

I reminded myself I was making the right decision. I wouldn't have to spend morbidly long daylight hours in Dullsville High. I'd have the ability to fly. And most important, I would be bonding with my true love, for all eternity.

I finally reached the coffin and stood alongside Alexander. He slid his white-gloved hand in mine, his plastic spider ring shining in the candlelight. He raised the pewter goblet to the moon and took a long drink. My heart raced as he passed it to me and I hesitantly lifted my veil from over my mouth. My hand was shaking, so the dark liquid wavered in the goblet.

"Maybe you aren't——," Alexander started, and put his hand over the glass.

"I am!" I argued defiantly. I pulled the goblet back and gulped the sweet, thick liquid.

I began to feel light-headed. The fog thickened around us. I could barely see Alexander's silhouette as he replaced the goblet on the coffin and then turned to me. With his white gloves, he gently lifted the black veil away from my face.

Now I could see clearly. Only I wasn't sure of what I was seeing. Instead of Alexander's usual long black hair, I noticed light-colored hair poking out from underneath his pallbearer's hat.

I gasped. It couldn't be!

"Jagger——," I exclaimed, frozen.

But when I looked into his eyes, I didn't see Alexander's rival's blue and green eyes that had once hypnotized me by the Mansion's gazebo. And they weren't the dark soulful eyes I had fallen in love with. These hypnotic eyes were green, and I'd seen them all my life.

"Trevor!" I declared, the words barely escaping my lips.

My childhood nemesis flashed a wicked grin,

two razor-sharp fangs hanging from his mouth.

I stepped back.

It was only last night at Dullsville's Spring Carnival that Alexander and I had tried to warn Trevor about Jagger's twin sister, Luna, who was looking to sink her newly formed fangs into the soccer snob's neck. Jagger had been seeking revenge on Alexander for not turning Luna into a vampire, and now that she'd been turned by another vampire, the nefarious teens were in Dullsville to find her a lifelong partner. But Trevor had failed to heed our warning. When Alexander and I arrived outside the Fun House and searched through the carnival, Trevor was gone.

Only now my nemesis had found me.

I tried to run, but Trevor grabbed my hand as I pulled away. "I've got you now, Monster Girl. Forever." He licked his lips and leaned into my neck.

I looked around for anything to help my escape. But when I reached out for the candelabra, I felt dizzy. Suddenly Trevor's mouth was on my neck.

"Get off!" I cried. "Let go of me!"

He pulled me into him with the force of a whole soccer team. I wedged my boot between us, and, with all my strength, I managed to push him away.

Trevor stumbled back and grabbed my arm. He tried to pull me close, but I bit his hand. I broke free as he stood up confidently and grinned a wicked smile. Blood began to drip from the corner of his mouth.

I reached for my neck. My palm felt warm and wet. I gasped. When I held my hand before me, it was covered in blood.

"No!" I cried.

Just then I saw a confused Alexander, also sporting a gray pallbearer's uniform, running up the cemetery aisle. I turned to Trevor, who just stood and smiled.

"Not you! Not for an eternity!" I yelled.

I sat up, screaming so hard my throat hurt.

I opened my eyes to darkness. I could hardly breathe. Where was I? In a coffin? A tomb? An empty grave?

Soft material covered my legs, but my eyes couldn't adjust to my surroundings. I figured I must be wrapped in a burial shroud.

My heart was throbbing. My skin perspiring. My mouth dry.

Flashing, bloodred numbers caught my eye: Two fifteen A.M.

I breathed a sigh of relief. I wasn't lying in an unknown coffin in Dullsville's cemetery but rather in my own bed.

Was I as safe as I thought? Maybe this was all part of my nightmare. My fingers shaking, I switched on my *Edward Scissorhands* lamp and ran to my dresser mirror. I closed my eyes, anticipating what I might *not* see. When I opened them, my ghostlike reflection stared back. I pulled my bed-head hair away from my shoulders and examined my neck.

My bedroom door flung open and my dad appeared in the doorway, sporting flannel boxers, a Lakers T-shirt, and messy hair. "What's wrong?" he asked, more annoyed than worried.

"Uh, nothing," I replied, startled. I dropped my hair and stepped away from the mirror.

"What happened?" my mom asked, barging in.

"I heard a scream," Billy Boy said, nosing his way behind them, his tired eyes heavy.

"I'm sorry I woke you guys. I just had a bad

dream," I confessed.

"You?" my father asked, raising his eyebrow. "I thought you loved bad dreams."

"I know. Can you believe it?" I asked, my heart still racing. "Who knew?"

"What was it about? You ran out of black lipstick?" Billy Boy teased.

"Yes. And I found a new one in *your* dresser drawer."

"Dad!" Billy Boy hollered, ready to pummel me.

"Now I know I'm not dreaming," I said, and playfully tousled my brother's hair.

"All right. Enough excitement for tonight. Let's all go back to sleep," my dad ordered, putting his arm around my brother as they left the room.

I settled back into bed.

"So what were you *really* dreaming about?" my mom asked curiously.

"It was nothing."

"Nothing woke up the whole house?" she asked.

She shook her head and started for the door.

"Mom . . . ," I said, my words stopping her.

"Does my neck look okay to you?" I whispered, pulling my hair back.

She returned to my bedside. "Looks like a regular neck to me," she said, examining it. "What were you expecting—a vampire bite?"

I gave her a quick smile. She pulled the covers over me as if I were still a child.

"I remember when you were a little girl and you stayed up all night with your father watching *Dracula* movies on our black-and-white TV," she reminisced fondly.

She handed me my Mickey Malice plush that had fallen beside my bed. "You never had nightmares then. It was as if you were comforted by vampires the way other kids are comforted by lullabies."

She kissed me on top of the head and reached for my lamp.

"Maybe you should leave it on," I said. "Just for tonight."

"Now you are scaring *me*," she said, and left my room.

2

The Almost Great Escape

The official welcome sign to my town should now read, "Welcome to Vampireville—come for a bite, but stay for an eternity!"

The town that I'd grown up in and had always called Dullsville was no longer dull. Not only was I dating a vampire, but now two other teen Nosferatus were living among Dullsvillians, whose biggest concern was getting the best price on the newest Prada purses or the latest Big Bertha golf clubs.

I was the only mortal who knew about the secret identity of the new bloodsucking inhabitants and I was dying to spill my guts to the *Dullsville Dispatch*. The front-page headline would read: GOTH GIRL GETS THE GOODS! Raven Madison Wins Nobel Peace Prize for Unearthing the Undead. Below, a color photograph would feature me standing next to Luna, Jagger, and Alexander—and I'd be the only one reflected in the picture.

If I came forward with my discoveries, my outcast life would be broadcast nationwide. I might be picked up in a chauffeur-driven hearse and my awaiting publicist would whisk me away on my Gulfstream jet for a media blitz tour; I'd be booked on CNN, *Oprah*, and MTV to plug my memoir, *Vampire Vixen*. My personal assistant would be in charge of making sure I had a bowl of black gummy bats and total darkness in the greenrooms at every talk show. My personal stylist would follow closely behind me, reapplying body tattoos, attaching blue hair extensions, and outfitting me in the latest Drac Blac dresses.

But in lieu of blabbing my discoveries to the world, I would have to keep Jagger's and Luna's ghastly secret to myself—that the twins were really vampires.

It had not always been so. Alexander shared with me that when the Maxwell twins were born, it was quickly discovered that Luna was not a vampire like everyone else in her family but rather a human—a genetic link that went back generations to a great-great mortal grandmother. A promise was made between the Sterlings and the Maxwells that on Luna's eighteenth birthday, Alexander was to meet Luna on sacred ground for a covenant ceremony—turning Luna into a vampire and bonding each to the other for eternity. When the day came, however, Alexander decided that Luna and he should both spend eternity with someone they love. After Alexander broke the two families' promise, Jagger sought revenge on Alexander. Once Luna was turned into a vampire by another vampire on unsacred ground, she joined her brother in Dullsville to meet a mortal teen with whom Luna could spend eternity. I knew that if I revealed the twins' true identity, then I'd be giving away Alexander's as well. I'd be putting my boyfriend in danger and could lose him forever.

So instead of being on the cover of *Gothic Girl*, I was going undercover.

The irony was that I'd have to convince Trevor, who had started the rumor in the first place that the Sterlings were vampires, that he had been right all along and now was in line to be the newest victim of Jagger and Luna's deadly duo. Though no one on earth repulsed me as much as Trevor, there was a gnawing inside me to warn him about the impending danger. And more important, if someone as wicked as Trevor became a vampire, all of Dullsville would be unsafe after sunset.

At Dullsville's drive-in, during the showing of *Kissing Coffins*, Alexander and I had tricked Jagger into believing I'd been bitten and turned into a vampiress. But several days later, at Dullsville's carnival, when Alexander and I confronted Luna in the Fun House's Hall of Mirrors, I was the only one whose image reflected. Would Jagger believe his sister or what his own eyes had witnessed at the drive-in?

"I'm not concerned," Alexander said, gently reassuring me that night when he pulled his butler Jameson's Mercedes into my driveway. "Jagger is seeking revenge on us through Trevor now. We can easily explain the Hall of Mirrors.

Besides, Jagger's ego is too big to admit he was double-crossed."

"So we should continue to keep up appearances that I am a vampire," I said. "It would be easier if we just go to the cemetery and you take my blood as your own."

Alexander turned off the engine.

I know he dreamed of being in my world as much as I dreamed of being in his. But when he turned to me, his shadowy eyes reflected the loneliness of living in a mysterious world that was filled with darkness and isolation.

As I gazed back at him, I wondered if I really wanted to be a part of a world that Alexander didn't want to be in. Was I just going through a phase that would seemingly last forever? At this point, it was irrelevant, as we sat parked in the driveway, on unsacred ground. Alexander was making the decision for us both, by saying nothing.

"Then I'll start just by ditching school," I thought aloud. "I'll replace my bed with a coffin, sleep in all day with the shades pulled, wake up just in time for dinner. We can feast on bloody steaks and party among the tombstones. I'm going to love being a vampire!"

He turned to me and placed his hand on my knee. "I've already caused you enough disruption by entering your life," he said softly. "First with Jagger, now with Luna. I'm not going to let this interfere with your family or school."

Frustrated, he pushed back his black hair, his earrings catching the moonlight.

"Don't say that—you've brought me a life I never knew existed. Adventure, belonging. True love."

His sullen eyes sparkled.

"Well, if you don't act normal, we'll have your parents, friends, and the whole town questioning your behavior," he argued.

I gnawed on my black fingernail. "But they already do."

A sweet smile came over his pale face. Then he furrowed his brow.

"Besides, you can do what I can't—attend school. That's where Trevor will be, if he's not already turned. Then you'll have a shot at convincing him to stay away from Luna."

I felt a sudden surge of pride. "You're entrusting me with a secret mission?"

"You'll be like a gothic Charlie's Angel."

"What if Jagger finds out I'm at school?" I asked. "He may wonder why I'm out in the daylight. I've never seen any vampires attending Dullsville High."

"That's the exact reason Jagger and Luna will never find out. Since they'll be hidden from the sun, they won't ever be able to see you," he reassured me.

"But what if Trevor or his soccer snob friends tell Jagger they saw me at school?" I pressed.

"They won't have proof," Alexander said with certainty. "Jagger isn't likely to believe what he hasn't seen. And he did see me bite you, or pretend to bite you," he admitted, "at the drive-in."

Alexander walked me to the door. He leaned in to me and gave me a long good-night kiss. "While you're at school, I'll be fast asleep dreaming of you."

Alexander blew me a kiss, got in his car, and drove down the driveway. When I turned to wave, he had already vanished from view.

That night, as I lay in bed, I tried to calm my anxious nerves. I closed my eyes and imagined Alexander alone in his attic bedroom, skillfully painting a portrait of us at Dullsville's carnival, blasting Korn from his stereo.

I wasn't sure Alexander could remain so calm, knowing Luna and Jagger were in Dullsville. After the sun rose, I wouldn't be able to see my vampire-mate until nightfall. As Alexander slept the day away, I would return to school and find Trevor on my own.

The next morning, I awoke to the sun scorching through the cracks between my curtains like a burning torch. I pulled the drapes tightly closed, covered myself with a blanket, and tried to go back to sleep. But I kept thinking about my mission—to save my nemesis from a thirsty vampiress.

I was in my bedroom scrounging for clothes for school when I heard the sound of a honking horn.

"Becky's here!" my mom called up to me from the kitchen.

"She's always ten minutes early!" I barked,

pulling black-and-white tights over my legs. My best friend had always kept farm hours, but now that she was dating Matt, Trevor's former silent shadow, she insisted on arriving at school even earlier.

The sound of a horn blasted again. "You'll see him for the next six hours!" I murmured to myself.

"Raven," my mom called again. "I can't take you in today. I have a meeting—"

"I know! I'll be down in a minute!"

The truth was if Alexander was waiting by the bleachers for me at Dullsville High each day, I'd set my *Nightmare Before Christmas* alarm clock for five thirty, too. But as I put on a black miniskirt and a torn *Donnie Darko* T-shirt, all I could think of was handsome Alexander sleeping in his darkened bedroom. I would face the sunny day without him.

As Becky impatiently honked again, I covered my already blackened, tired eyes with charcoal eye shadow and eyeliner. Finally I grabbed my backpack and waved to my mom, and climbed into Becky's truck.

"I'm disconnecting that horn immediately," I

said in a grumpy tone as I climbed into Becky's pickup.

"I'm sorry, Raven, it's just that—"

"I know, I know. 'I'm meeting Matt by the bleachers before school.'"

"Am I getting annoying?" she asked.

"I'd be the same way if Alexander was waiting for me at school, instead of Trevor Mitchell."

"Thanks for understanding."

Becky passed a yellow bus loaded with preteen students heading for Dullsville Middle. Several students gathered at their windows. Some gawked at me, while the others pointed and laughed. I would have been surprised and perturbed, except that they did that every day.

"Well, speaking of Trevor . . . I have some major dirt on him."

"What's the buzz factor?"

"On a scale of one to ten, it's a nine and a half."

"Bring it on," I said, checking my ghoulish makeup in her broken visor mirror.

"Trevor has a girlfriend."

"You mean Luna?" I said, slamming the visor back.

"Luna?" she asked, confused.

"I mean, luna . . . tic. She's got to be a lunatic to date him. Anyway, who told you?"

"Matt said Trevor was seen with a goth at the carnival. I thought he meant you until he said she had ghost white hair."

"Goth? That's what people are saying about her?"

She nodded her head. "Yes. And that she's a major hottie. Matt didn't say that, of course, but he said that's what the soccer snobs are saying. You know how guys are, checking out the new girl."

"But Trevor despises anyone not sporting school colors."

"Yeah, but she dotes on him like he's a prince. She and her brother worship him. So it's like he's captain of the soccer snobs *and* the goths. His head is going to explode.

"He probably likes her," she went on, "but it's you he really loves. It's obvious he's had a crush on you since you were kids. He can't have you, so he's trying to get second best."

I rolled my eyes and pretended to gag. "Thanks for the compliment," I said sarcastically.

"The good news is maybe Trevor will stop torturing you."

If Trevor became a vampire, his bite would be worse than his bark.

"Apparently she showed up at their soccer practice last night, cheering for Trevor," Becky continued.

"She did? I was afraid this would happen."

"Afraid of what?"

"Uh . . . ," I began, stalling. "That Trevor would be popular again. After we've worked so hard to expose his inner monster."

"Without Matt by his side, no one cares what he says or does anymore."

"But who knows what . . ."

"We have our own lives now," Becky said proudly. "So who cares if he has one too."

I looked out the window and reflected on the rivalry Trevor and I had had since childhood. Deep down, I knew Becky was right, but I felt torn. Even though I detested Trevor and I was in love with Alexander, there was still a teeny competitive part of me that didn't want Trevor to be popular and have a girlfriend—vampire or not.

Becky and I arrived late at the soccer field and spotted Matt walking down the bleachers, listening to his iPod. Becky raced over to him as if he had just disembarked off a military vessel.

I reached the slobbering pair. "Eh hem!" I said, coughing, and tapped Becky on the shoulder.

They broke apart their superglued embrace.

"Becky tells me Trevor has a girlfriend," I blurted out.

"I didn't say that," Matt said, looking strangely at Becky.

"But Becky said a girl was at practice rooting for Trevor."

"I guess. I thought you were done with him."

"I am, but gossip is gossip. Did Trevor leave with her?" I asked.

"She was with a creepy guy in a black knit hat. I think you'd like him. Pale with a lot of tattoos. When the team came out of the locker room, they had already gone."

Matt adjusted his backpack, grabbed Becky's hand, and started heading for school.

"Wait—did Trevor look different?" I interrogated.

"He wasn't wearing any tattoos," Matt said with a laugh.

"No, I mean unusually pale. Really thirsty. Redder eyes."

He thought for a moment. "He said he wasn't feeling well," he remembered. "Why all this interest in Trevor?"

The smitten couple looked at me curiously, waiting for an answer.

Suddenly the bell rang.

"I'd love to stay and chat, but you know how I like to be punctual," I lied, and took off.

During my first three classes I was preoccupied with confronting Trevor, so to distract myself I daydreamed about Alexander. I wrote our names in my journal—Raven Madison x Alexander Sterling, TRUE LOVE ALWAYS—surrounded by black roses.

When the lunch bell finally rang, I skipped meeting Becky and Matt at the bleachers. Instead I combed the campus searching for Trevor.

I couldn't find my nemesis on the soccer field, the gym, or the steps where all the soccer snobs ate their filet mignon baguettes.

"Where's Trevor?" I asked a cheerleader who was tying her sneaker.

She eyeballed my outfit with contempt. She glared at me as if she were a queen and I were a serf who had dared to stumble upon her castle. She picked up her red and white pom-poms and turned away as if she had already wasted too much time.

"Have you seen Trevor?" I repeated.

"He's home," she snarled.

"You mean I could have stayed home too?" I mumbled. The only reason I came to school today was to find him.

She rolled her eyes at me.

I glared back, imagining what it would be like if I was a real vampire. I'd transform into a spooky bat, swoop around her as she let out a bloodcurdling scream, and tangle myself in her perfectly combed blond hair.

"Duh. He's sick," she finally said, scrutinizing me as if I, too, were spreading contagions.

Sick? Matt said that last night Trevor was pale and wasn't feeling well. My mind raced. Sick from what? The sunlight? Garlic? Maybe Luna and Jagger had already managed to lure him to

Dullsville's cemetery. Right now Trevor could be sleeping in a red and white coffin.

I had to act fast.

I'd spent most of my life sneaking in and out of places—my house, the Mansion, Dullsville's elementary and middle schools. But since I was still a mere mortal and did not yet possess the powers of a shapeshifting bat, Dullsville High was getting harder to just walk, climb, or tunnel out of.

Principal Reed hired security guards to patrol both entrances of the campus, cutting down on kids leaving for lunch and not returning to school. Dullsville High was becoming like Alcatraz. All that remained was for the school board to encircle the campus with frigid water and killer sharks.

Instead of sneaking out, I'd have to make my exit known.

I opened Nurse William's office door to find three other kids wheezing, coughing, and sneezing in the waiting room, glaring at me as if I were the one who was ill.

I realized this might take longer than waiting until school let out.

I jotted down notes in my Olivia Outcast journal when Nurse William, the poster woman for health, bounced out. Exposed to seasonal colds, allergies, and excuses, Nurse William was impervious to dripping noses. Looking more like she stepped out of a gym than an examination room, she could probably snap off her own blood pressure band with a single bicep curl.

"Teddy Lerner," she called, reading from a chart. "It's your turn," she said, flashing a Colgate smile.

"I need to see you immediately," I interjected, standing up and holding my stomach. "I don't think I can wait much longer."

Teddy stared at me, his nose as red as Rudolph's, and sneezed. I almost felt bad, but I knew all Teddy needed was a big Kleenex and a bowl of chicken soup. If I didn't get to Trevor Mitchell soon, there might not be any blood left to draw in town.

"All right, Raven."

Nurse William, like Principal Reed, knew me on a first-name basis, since I'd been to each of their offices on numerous occasions.

I followed her into her office—a small, sterile room with the usual jars of tongue depressors, Band-Aids, extra long Q-tips, and a blue cot.

I sat on a metal chair next to Nurse William's desk.

"I've had the chills since I woke up," I fibbed.

She examined my eyes with a small pen light.

"Uh-huh," she said.

She held up her stethoscope.

"Take a deep breath," she said, putting her instrument on my chest.

I slowly breathed in and then fake sneezed and coughed so wildly, I thought I'd pulled a lung.

She quickly drew back the stethoscope.

"Interesting."

Nurse William opened her glass cabinet and pulled out an ear thermometer and sterile cover and took my temperature.

After a minute, she read the results.

"Just what I thought."

"I'm sick?"

"I think you have a case of either 'testitis' or 'I Didn't Do My Homework Syndrome.' It's common in the spring."

"But I feel awful!"

"You probably just need a good night's rest."

"I think I need to go home," I choked out. "You are keeping me against my will. I have a stomachache and headache, and my throat hurts," I said, talking through my nose.

"We can't release you unless you have a fever," she said, returning the thermometer to the glass cabinet.

"Haven't you heard of preventive medicine?"

"You do look like you haven't slept. Well, you'll have to get approval from Principal Reed," she said with a sigh, exhausted.

Great. New rules to be broken.

I stepped into Principal Reed's office with a note from Nurse William.

I fake sneezed and coughed.

"You've used up all your school sick days," he said, perusing my file. "You've requested to leave school one hundred and thirty days out of the one hundred and forty days of school so far."

"So thirty-one might be the magic number?"

"Well, you do look awful," he finally said, and signed my school release form.

"Thanks!" I said sarcastically.

I wasn't planning on appearing so convincing.

"I'm sorry, Raven," my mom said as she pulled our SUV into the driveway. "I feel terrible leaving you alone, but I have an off-site meeting that's been scheduled for months."

She walked me to the front door and gave me a quick hug as I stepped inside.

"Funny," I began. "I'm feeling better already."

I closed the door, and as soon as I saw my mom drive down the street, I grabbed my usual vampire detectors—garlic powder and a compact mirror belonging to Ruby White of Armstrong Travel—and headed straight for Trevor's.

No wonder vampires didn't venture out in daylight. I hungered for the safe haven of shade from trees and hovering clouds and thirsted for the warm blanket of nightfall. The hot sun began to bake my pale skin as I rode my bike up the Mitchells' driveway and passed a Ferguson and Son's Painting pickup parked in front of their four-car garage. I laid the bike against the side of the screened-in porch and rang the Mitchells' bell. Their dog began to bark from the backyard.

When no one answered, I rang the bell again.

Suddenly a small, elderly white-haired man carrying a ladder came out of the garage.

"Hi, Mr. Ferguson," I said, running over to the familiar painter. "Is Trevor home?"

The elderly worker looked at me oddly.

"It's me, Raven," I said, pulling down my shades.

"Hi, Raven. Shouldn't you be at school?" he wondered.

"I'm on lunch break," I replied.

"I didn't think they let kids go home for lunch anymore. In my day, there was no such thing as school lunch," he began. "We had to—"

"Really, I'd love to hear all about it, but I don't have much time—"

"I just dispatched my sons for takeout. If I'd known you were coming . . . ," he began politely.

"That's very sweet of you, but I just need to see Trevor."

"It's probably not a good day for a visit. He's been in his room since sunrise."

Sunrise? I wondered.

"Well, I'll just be a minute," I said, walking past him toward the garage.

Mr. Ferguson put down the ladder.

"Raven, I can't let you in."

"But why? It's only me—," I whined.

Didn't he know I was on a mission to save Dullsville?

"Not when I'm on a job. It could cost me my contract."

More rules to be broken.

I plastered on my best puppy-dog face, the one I used with my dad when I wanted to stay out late. But the old man was steadfast. "The Mitchells should be home after five."

"I'll come back later then," I responded. "It was nice seeing you."

I walked over to my bike as Mr. Ferguson awkwardly carried the ladder to his truck. With his back to me, I knew I had only seconds. I dashed into the garage, snuck past a vintage Bentley, and opened the door to the laundry room. The smell of fresh paint wafted through the house as I raced over the plastic drop cloth, past the newly painted sunflower yellow kitchen. I would have complimented Mr. Ferguson on his paint job if it wouldn't have given away my dubious location.

I ran toward the front hall.

I'd been to Trevor's house only once, for his fifth birthday party, and that was only because he had invited everyone in our kindergarten class. My parents always told me that when they grew up and returned to their childhood homes, the houses looked smaller. Well, if Trevor's house seemed like a castle when I was in kindergarten, then as a sophomore, it had only downsized to a mansion. Mr. Mitchell owned half of Dullsville, and Mrs. Mitchell made her living by serial shopping. And it showed.

The entranceway alone seemed three stories high. A marble balcony was accentuated with two descending bleach white wooden staircases forming a semicircle around an indoor fountain. A grand dining room sat off to the left with a white diamond teardrop chandelier and a glass table with twelve beige linen-covered chairs. It was almost the same style as the living room at the Mansion—but without the cobwebs. On the right, a sitting room the size of my house was decorated in African art and adorned with enough fertility statues to impregnate an entire country.

I remembered standing in this exact spot when I was five, just after my mom dropped me off. For what seemed like hours, my classmates were running past me, giggling as if I weren't even there.

Finally we were called outside to the Mitchells' football-size backyard where a clown, a merry-go-round, and a pony were awaiting us. Watching my classmates dance, sing, and ride, I sat alone on the patio until Trevor opened one perfectly wrapped present after another containing Hot Wheels, LEGOs, or Nerf footballs. Then Mrs. Mitchell handed him a black box complete with a black bow, wrapped by yours truly.

Trevor ripped the package open and pulled out a brand-new mint-condition Dracula action figure. His eyes lit up and he exclaimed, "Wow!"

Mrs. Mitchell cued him to "show and share."

Wide-eyed, he proudly passed it to the pig-tailed partygoer sitting next to him.

"That looks like Raven!" the girl shouted.

"Gross. It probably has cooties," another warned, returning it to him.

Trevor's gorgeous smile turned into a hideous frown. He glared at me and threw my gift back in the box.

I remained alone on the patio steps for the rest of the party while the other kids ate cake and ice cream.

My stomach turned as I remembered that day. I paused for a moment and wondered if instead of running up to Trevor's room and warning him about Luna's intentions, I should sneak back out the way I came in.

I heard the laundry room doorknob turn.

I quietly raced up the pristine staircase and past more doors than were in the MGM Grand Hotel. After peeking in a million guest bedrooms and bathrooms down a hallway the length of an international runway, one final door awaited.

I'm not sure what I expected to find—Trevor had been sleeping since sunrise. It had been confirmed by several sources that he was sick and pale. If Trevor had already been bitten, I was putting myself in danger.

I had no other choice. I double-checked the garlic stashed in my purse.

I knocked gently.

When I didn't get a response, I slowly twisted the handle and opened the door. I took off my glasses and my hood. I crept inside.

Light from the hallway shined softly through the bedroom. The dark curtains were drawn closed—one sign Trevor could already be turned.

The soccer snob must have had his own personal interior decorator. His bedroom could have graced the cover of *Architectural Digest Teen*.

Next to the curtains, a giant flat-screen computer sat on a white modular desk. On one side of the room was a wall-mounted gazillion-inch plasma TV. Underneath it was a teen's dream lounge—a red futon couch, a soccer-themed pinball machine, and a foosball table.

Lastly and most ghastly was his midnight blue king-size bed with a soccer-goal headboard.

I almost gagged.

I could see Trevor's golden blond hair sticking out from underneath his comforter.

As much as I would have liked to short-sheet his bed or stick his hand in warm water, I decided to open his computer desk to search for any hidden clues. All I found were unsharpened pencils, a school lock, and loose batteries.

I opened two shutter doors, which led to something more like a sporting goods store than a teen's closet. A few feet away a glass bookshelf was adorned with a million soccer trophies and medals, and on the wall hung ribbons, a half dozen framed soccer pictures, and *Dullsville High Chatterbox* articles. I glided my finger across a dust-free gold trophy when I noticed something dust-filled hidden behind it—a decade-old Dracula action figure.

For a moment I almost felt a warming sensation filter through my icy veins. Then he stirred.

I quietly tiptoed over to him. I stood frozen. The normally sun-kissed soccer snob looked like one of the undead. But even when he was sick, Trevor was gorgeous. It almost made me ill that he had gotten so much by having a pretty face and a fast kick to midfield.

I wondered why this conservative snob was so attracted to the gothic Luna. Was it because she was pursuing him? Was it to get back at me? Or had my nemesis found the true love of his life? The major issue that perplexed me was why I cared.

I opened my purse and pulled out Ruby's compact. My fingers quavering, I angled it toward Trevor. All at once, he turned over and knocked it out of my hand. I scrambled on the floor to find it.

"What's going on?" he asked, his voice hoarse.

I curled up alongside his bed, breathing the shallowest of breaths.

"Jasper? Is that you?" he asked.

I lifted up his blue duvet so I could squeeze underneath his bed. Instead of an open space to hide, I found a handle to a king-size trundle drawer—as if he didn't have enough closet space.

I had nowhere to escape. I'd have to switch to plan B.

"Hi, Trevor," I said, popping up.

Startled, the soccer snob let out a scraggly yell. "What the hell are you doing here?" he shouted, sitting up.

"I just—," I stammered, fumbling with the compact and trying to shove it back into my purse.

"How did you get in?"

"Your nanny let me in," I teased. "I'm not surprised you still have one."

"What are you doing in my room?" Trevor wondered, fingering his tousled blond hair.

"I heard you were sick."

"So?"

"I wanted to know if you needed anything."

"Are you insane?"

"I'm fulfilling my health class assignment: Help someone in need."

"But I'm not in need, especially from you."

"I'll be the judge of that. I think you should start with some sunshine," I said, like a gothic Mary Poppins. "I'm the only one who likes it this gloomy." I went to his window and pulled back the heavy drapes.

"Stop!" he said, shielding his eyes.

But I continued to draw the curtains as far as they could go.

"Get out of here, freak!" he hollered, squinting.

I waited to see if there was any reaction. He could recoil. Maybe he'd melt.

I got a reaction from Trevor all right, but it wasn't what I expected. He got up, his pale face now flushed with anger.

"Get out already," he ordered. "Go back to the troll hole you live in. You've contaminated my house enough already."

I grabbed the garlic container from my purse and held it out to him.

"What's that?" he asked.

"Garlic. It helps clear out the system. Why don't you breathe it in," I said, stepping closer.

"Get that away from me, you freak."

Trevor didn't recoil like Alexander had when I accidentally exposed him to garlic powder. Instead, Trevor got madder.

I pulled out a pen and a Hello Batty paper pad. "Now," I said like a nurse filling out a patient's records, "have you kissed anyone in the past forty-eight hours?"

"What's it your business?"

"I have to fill out a communicable diseases questionnaire. You don't want your new girl-friend, Luna, to get your diseases, do you?"

"Why, are you jealous?"

"Of course not," I replied with a laugh.

"That's what this is really about," he said, his raspy tone suddenly brightening. "Why you are here, in my house. In my room—," he said, step-ping closer.

"Don't flatter yourself—"

"You couldn't handle seeing me with Luna—," he said with a smile.

"Frankly, I can't handle seeing you at all."

"I knew it. I saw it in your eyes at the carnival," he said, taking another step toward me.

"That's not what you saw in my eyes."

I tried to get a quick glance at both sides of his neck. But he mistook the reason for my gaze. He stepped toward me and leaned in to kiss me.

I held him at bay with my pad of paper.

"Get off!"

"But I thought that's why you came—"

I rolled my eyes. "I need to know—have you been bitten by anything or anyone?"

"Of course not. But I won't tell if you don't tell," he said with a clever grin.

"Then my work is complete," I said, racing for the door. "Now take two dog biscuits and don't call me in the morning."

Trevor stood still, weary and confused.

"And most important," I offered as I opened the door, "stay away from the cemetery."

"I'm sick," he said. "Not dead."

I hopped on my bike. Coasting back home, I

was relieved that Trevor wasn't a vampire—for the town's sake and for mine.

As the sun set, I lay in bed under the covers.

"I hate to leave you again," my mom said, "but they are honoring your father at the country club. It's been such a busy day, I feel like I'm neglecting you."

"I feel tons better. I took a nap and I'm totally recovered."

"Well, Billy is over at Henry's. We'll pick him up after the ceremony."

As soon as I heard my dad's BMW pull out of the driveway, I jumped out of bed, fully dressed, and headed over to the Mansion.

I found Alexander in his attic room. He was staring pensively out the window. When I tapped at his door, his mood quickly changed. He gave me a long hello kiss, and for a moment I forgot all about my childhood nemesis and a lurking vampiress named Luna.

"We have to do something," Alexander said suddenly. I was quickly pulled from a heavenly cloud nine and back into the threat of the Underworld.

"I can think of a few things. Shall we stay in here?" I teased coyly. "Or take our party to the gazebo?"

But Alexander didn't smile. "I'm serious," he said.

I missed Alexander so desperately during the day, I felt grateful to be with him now. Though I was excited by the adventures of the town I now called "Vampireville," I also resented that Jagger and Luna took romantic time away from Alexander and me.

"But now that we're together, it's hard for me to think of anything but you. I've been waiting all day to see you," I said.

"I know, me too," he said with a sigh. "But until Jagger and Luna are gone, we can't sit around. Did you see Trevor?"

"Yes," I began, sitting in his beat-up comfy chair. "He was sick today and stayed home from school."

"Sick?" he asked, worried. "Is it already too late?"

"No," I said. "Fortunately Luna hasn't sunk her fangs into him yet. He just has the flu."

"Great!" he said, relieved, and leaned on the

arm of the chair. Then he turned serious. "If he was home sick, how did you see him?"

"Uh . . . ," I stammered, turning away.

"You didn't," he said in a scornful voice.

"Well—"

"You went to his house? Alone?" he asked, glaring down at me.

"No, the painter was there," I said, fiddling with a loose string from the fabric of the chair.

Alexander knelt down and took my hand. "Raven—I don't want you to be alone with him. If Trevor isn't a vampire, he is still a vulture."

"I know. You are right," I replied, his dark eyes melting me.

When my mom and dad were protective of me, it was annoying; when it came from Alexander, it was sexy.

"Promise me—"

"I promise," I said.

"Well, if they didn't get to Trevor already, then they must be waiting for the right moment."

"That would be ironic. Trevor, who hates anything goth, gets to be a vampire, and I, who would love nothing more, don't."

"It is important to be whoever you are, for

the right reason," he said, stroking my hand reassuringly.

"I know."

"Besides," he began, rising and returning to the attic window, "Trevor has no idea what Luna has in store for him."

I followed him and nestled in the dusty window seat. "What do we do?" I asked.

"Somehow we have to force them to go back to Romania."

"With an iron stake?" I wondered. "Or a fiery torch?"

Alexander shook his head, still thinking.

"Maybe I could swing a discounted fare from Ruby at Armstrong Travel," I suggested, pulling at a tear on my black leather boot. "We could convince Jagger and Luna that their parents miss them and demand their immediate return."

"But at this point we don't even know where they are," he said, frustrated. "They're hiding somewhere in the shadows."

"If we can take away the shadows, then we take away their defense," I said.

"You're right," he agreed suddenly.

"I am?" I asked, excited by my unlikely

genius. "How do we take away a shadow?"

"Not a shadow . . . ," he said, scooching next to me. "We have to take away the one thing that makes Jagger safe, no matter where he is."

I looked at Alexander curiously.

"The one thing that protects him from humans, other vampires, and the sun," he continued.

"Yes?" I asked eagerly.

"We have to find Jagger's coffin."

"Wow. That's perfect. Then he won't have anywhere to hide."

Alexander smiled, exhilarated that we finally had a plan.

"But wait," I said. "Can't Jagger just sleep in a bed like you, with the shades drawn? Or hide in the loft of a barn? You don't sleep in a coffin."

Alexander looked at me with deep, almost shameful eyes.

Then he rose and pushed aside his beat-up comfy chair, revealing a small attic door. He reached into his back pocket and pulled out a skeleton key.

"I do," he whispered.

He unlocked the bolt and slowly opened the

door, and we stepped inside a dark, dusty ancient hideaway.

There, sitting in the shadows, was a secret in the shape of a casket—a simple black coffin, with dirt haphazardly sprinkled around it. Next to it was a wooden table with an unlit half-melted candle and a small, softly painted portrait of me.

"I had no idea—," I said with barely any breath.

"You weren't supposed to."

"But your bed—it's always unmade."

"It's where I rest and try to dream that I am like you."

I grabbed his hand and held it close. "You never had to hide anything in your world from me," I said, looking up into his lonely eyes.

"I know," he said. "I was hiding it from myself."

Alexander closed and locked the small attic door, once again concealing his conflicted true identity.

T o find a vampire, you have to think like a vampire," Alexander said, grabbing his backpack. "I won't be gone more than an hour." He gave me a quick kiss.

"Gone?" I asked, following him toward his bedroom door.

"You'll have to stay here. I'm going to sacred ground."

"I'm going with you. If Jagger thinks I'm a vampire, then I'll be safe," I argued.

"And if he doesn't?"

"Then I have this." I pulled out my container

of garlic powder from my purse.

Alexander quickly retreated.

"It's tightly sealed," I said, referring to the time it spilled out in my purse, causing Alexander to have an allergic reaction and forcing me to inject him with an antidote. "I'll wait outside," I pleaded.

Alexander paused. He wiped his flopping rock-star hair away from his gorgeous face and slung his backpack on his shoulder. He glanced at the door, then back at me. Finally he held his pale hand out. While it was hard enough to be separated during the daylight, it was unbearable during the moonlight. As Alexander and I walked down the windy streets and toward the cemetery, I realized it was a dream come true—to be walking with one vampire and searching for another.

I'd never seen anyone in the moonlight as handsome as Alexander, vampire or not. His pale face seemed to glow, and his smile seemed to illuminate what the moon and the stars couldn't.

"Where are we going?" I finally asked.

"Your favorite place."

"My favorite place is here—by your side."

"Mine too," he said, squeezing my hand.

"Will Jagger know I'm still mortal?"

"It's not written on your forehead, is it?" he teased.

As he led me to an unknown destination, he walked with an air of confidence and determination I hadn't seen before.

We arrived at the entrance to Dullsville's cemetery.

"Remember when Old Jim took our tickets at the carnival, he accused you of sleeping at the cemetery?" he asked.

"But I wasn't," I defended. "I haven't done that in months!"

"I know. So if it's not you, then who do you think it is?" he asked.

I answered like an eager student. "Jagger."

"Trevor is safe for the night—but we're not." Then he paused. "You better stay outside the cemetery," he warned, changing his mind about our plan. "It's sacred ground and you would be in danger."

"You mean you bring me to the scene of the crime and don't let me dust for fingerprints? Or at least leave any?"

"You'll be safe only if you remain on the

outside." He tenderly brushed my hair away from my face.

As Alexander climbed over the gate, I reluctantly stayed behind. I anxiously dug my boot into the wet grass, feeling as if I were being left out of the adventure of a lifetime. What could I accomplish by staying behind? Alexander and I could cover more terrain if there were two of us searching the graveyard. Besides, if Jagger still thought I was a vampire, it would be more natural for me to be standing inside a cemetery than outside one.

I could barely see Alexander's shrinking silhouette in the distance. Then I quickly climbed the gate and jogged after him.

I ran among the tombstones, as quiet as a wandering ghost following Alexander's shadowy figure.

As I approached him, I realized the figure I was running to was a monument.

I didn't see Alexander anywhere.

"Alexander?" I called.

I wondered where he could have disappeared to so quickly. He must have turned behind the caretaker's shed.

I raced around to the back of the shed, but

all I saw was an abandoned shovel.

"Alexander?" I called again.

I continued to walk in the direction of the baroness's monument. Maybe Alexander was paying his respects to his grandmother as he searched the graveyard. When I approached the monument, however, the only thing visiting the stone memorial was a curious squirrel.

I walked on. Underneath a weeping willow tree, I saw a newly dug grave. I carefully walked toward it when I noticed a familiar pattern of dirt. Gravediggers make piles, not circles. I tip-toed closer. Jagger's stickered coffin could be lying inside, Jagger himself sitting on top, waiting for a mortal to be lured into his trap. I took a deep breath and peered down.

The grave was empty. No stickered coffin. No fang-toothed teen of darkness.

Where was Jagger? And more important, where was Alexander? I was standing in the middle of three acres of sacred ground. I'd picnicked alone a million times at Dullsville's cemetery, feeling as comfortable as if it were my own home. Tonight, though, I realized I'd perhaps made the biggest mistake of my life. Alexander had been right when he told me to stay outside the cemetery's gates. If Jagger was lurking in the shadows, he could easily sink his fangs into me before my true love had a chance to realize I was no longer standing by the graveyard's entrance.

My heart began to throb. My blood pressure soared.

I did have some mace, but I wasn't sure it would work against teen vampires.

I stuck my hand in my purse and clutched the container of garlic powder in my sweaty fingers and tiptoed through the tombstones.

"Alexander?" I whispered.

The howling wind was the only audible sound.

I turned around and could barely see the entrance to the cemetery. If I ran at top speed, I could reach the safety of the gate, though I wasn't sure I could outrun a flying vampire bat.

There was no other choice.

I took a deep breath, but as I took my first step, a strong hand bore down on my shoulder.

"Let go!" I cried.

I turned around to pry it off with one hand and aim the garlic container with the other.

"Don't!" a voice shouted.

I froze.

"What are you doing here?" Alexander asked sternly. "I told you to wait by the entrance."

"But I found something—an empty grave encircled with dirt."

"I did too," he said. "And I discovered something else."

I followed Alexander toward the back of the cemetery to a lone, dead sycamore. A brown package was sitting at the foot of the tree. Alexander picked up the package and held it in front of me. In crooked handwriting was marked: Jagger Maxwell.

The upper-left-hand corner was stamped: COFFIN CLUB.

It was the nocturnal gothic club where I'd first encountered Jagger.

The box had been ripped open, as if severed with razor-sharp teeth. Alexander pulled back the flaps and showed me the contents. It was a vampire's treasure chest: a box full of crystal, pewter, and silver amulets, filled with the sweet red nectar vampires crave. Fresh off the necks of the Coffin Club clubsters, who I'd seen wearing their blood as innocent charms, these vials now in turn were serving as a teen vampire's nourishment.

"Without a Coffin Club to hide in," Alexander explained, "Jagger could be chased out of town quickly. He couldn't make his presence known. This was his only means of survival."

Alexander eyed the amulets like a child eyeing a gumball machine. Instead of returning the box underneath the tree, he stuck it in his backpack.

"Should we wait here until he comes back?"

Alexander grabbed my hand. "He's not coming back."

"How do you know?"

"There is only one empty grave. He needs two now."

As we quickly walked through the cemetery, I imagined Jagger sitting underneath the dead tree, secluded in the back of the cemetery, waiting for Luna to arrive from Romania. He would be tipping back several amulets, like the tiny bottles of liquor anxious travelers sip on airplanes, while he plotted her visit and their next location.

"Shouldn't we continue searching for Luna?" I asked Alexander as we approached my house on our way back from Dullsville's cemetery. I wasn't ready for my vampire hunting to end.

But instead of walking hand in hand with Alexander, his hands were buried in his pockets. He seemed unusually cold and distant.

"I think your cemetery searching days are over," he said sternly.

"You're mad at me for not listening?" I asked, sincerely concerned.

Alexander stopped and turned to me. "You put yourself in grave danger. I only want you to be safe."

"But if Jagger thinks I am a vampire, I was safer in the cemetery," I said, attempting to cozy up to him.

"You may be right. But . . ." He folded his arms, leaned against a parked SUV, and looked toward the moon.

It was one thing to push my parents over the edge with my princess of darkness wardrobe, or to stay out past curfew, or even to boss Becky into climbing over the Mansion's gate or to convince her to sneak into movies, but I'd never felt as rotten as I now did, disappointing the one person who meant the most to me.

"I should have listened," I admitted.

He put his hands back in his oversized pockets and avoided eye contact.

"I want so badly to be a part of your world," I said, knitting my arms through his. "I want to taste the adventure alongside you."

Alexander softened and gently stroked my hair. "You are already a part of my world," he said with a smile that lit up his pale face. "You know that. I'm just asking you to be careful."

"I understand. I just don't want us to be apart—even for a moment. But I'll try harder."

Alexander grabbed my hand and we continued down the street, past houses, trees, and mailboxes.

"Okay now, I have to come up with a plan," he said.

"Plan? I'm all about plans! Where do we start?"

Alexander looked buried in thought and led me toward my house.

"I still want to hang out," I whined. "Darkness is our only time together," I continued, staring up into his midnight eyes.

"I know, but—"

"And daylight seems like an eternity without you. I have to endure unbearably boring teachers, classmates who ostracize me, and two yuppie parents who don't get black lipstick."

"I feel the same," he revealed, stopping at the bottom of my driveway. "Except for me it's not daylight, but starlight and moonlight. During the long midnight hours, I hang out underneath your window and imagine what you're dreaming of. I used to thrive in the darkness; now I almost resent it."

Alexander and I walked up my driveway. Instead of taking the path that led to my front door, Alexander escorted me toward my backyard.

"Yay! We can't let Jagger spoil our night," I cheered.

"We do have to be careful," he warned. "But you're right. I'm not ready to say good-bye just yet," he confessed. "Not now, not ever."

Suddenly a motion detector light above the garage triggered, illuminating the driveway, Billy Boy's basketball hoop, Mom's SUV, and a mortal girl and her vampire boyfriend.

"No!" Alexander shouted. He quickly shielded

his pale face and retreated into the shadows.

"Are you all right?" I called, squinting into the darkness.

Alexander didn't answer. I followed him into the grass, toward our east-side neighbor's fence.

It took a moment for my eyes to adjust, though I still couldn't see him. "Alexander, where are you? Are you hurt?"

I heard a fluttering above the power lines behind me. I followed the sound, which continued back over the driveway in the opposite direction from where I had been standing. When I walked through my backyard, there was a rustling in the bushes by our west-side neighbor's fence. Alexander was standing in front of them.

"How did you get over here so fast?" I asked curiously, all the while knowing the answer. "That was cool. It's like dating a superhero."

Alexander dusted off his black jeans, unfazed by his unearthly abilities.

"Are you okay?" I asked. Before he could answer, I was in his arms.

"Now that you are with me," he said, caressing my hair.

"I forgot—"

"I didn't melt," he said. "I can handle softer light, like candles or lamps. But a burst of high-powered light repels me."

"I didn't even think—," I began when he pulled back and placed his frosty white index finger on my black lips.

"I'll be able to think better out here," he said, and stared up to the sky. "With you, underneath the stars. We don't have much time."

He led me over to the rickety wooden swing set Billy Boy and I had outgrown but my parents hadn't bothered to get rid of.

"It's been an eternity since I've hung out here," I told him. I could feel my pale face flush, exhilarated that I was finally able to share a place I'd spent in childhood isolation. "I used to bury my Barbies over there," I said, pointing to a mound of soil underneath an oak tree.

We each sat on a faded yellow plastic swing.

I began swinging, but Alexander remained still. He picked up twigs and threw them into the bushes, as if he were tossing Jagger out of Dullsville.

I skidded my combat boots into the weathered patches of grass.

"What's wrong?" I asked, now standing before him.

Alexander pulled me close. "It's hard for me to relax, knowing Jagger and Luna are still plotting revenge."

"Well, let's think like them. If he isn't in a cemetery and we don't have a Coffin Club in Dullsville, where could they be?"

"I know we are both vampires, but our instincts are different. He sees the world in black and red—*blood* red. I see the world in all different colors."

I grabbed his icy hand and fingered his spider ring.

"Just because you and Jagger are vampires doesn't mean you are the same. Look at Trevor and me. We're human, but total opposites," I reassured him.

Alexander broke into a smile. "I just want to be spending the darkness with you; instead I'm thinking of *him*."

"That's my fault," I insisted. "I wish I hadn't gone to the Coffin Club. Then we'd never be in this mess. I led Jagger right to you, and Luna straight to Trevor."

"You had nothing to do with this. If I'd said yes to Luna at the covenant ceremony in Romania, none of this would have happened."

"Then we wouldn't be together. And that is the most important thing."

"You're right," he said, and pulled me onto his lap. "But now we have a couple of vampires to catch."

We gently swung back and forth on the swing. The stars shone in the night sky. The sweet smell of Drakar filled the air. The crickets seemed to be singing for us.

Just then my bedroom light switched on.

"Who's in my room?" I snarled.

Billy Boy jumped in front of the window, with his back toward us, hugging himself. From our vantage point, he appeared as if he were making out with a girl.

Alexander laughed at my little brother's antics.

"Get out of my room!" I yelled.

Billy Boy held Nightmare in his hands and waved her paw at me.

"Let her go! You'll give her fleas!" I shouted.

"He just wants your attention," Alexander

said, dragging his boots into the dirt and holding one arm around me like a safety belt. "It's cute. He adores you."

"Adores me?"

"He has the coolest sister ever."

I turned to Alexander and gave him a long kiss. I'd spent my whole life as an outsider. Even though Alexander and I had been dating for a few months, it was still hard to get used to the fact that anyone would think I was normal, much less cool.

"It's getting late," he said. He grabbed my hand and began walking me to the front door. "You get your rest while I figure out where Jagger is."

"The night has just begun," I argued.

"Not for someone who has classes at eight in the morning."

"They always go on without me," I said with a shrug.

Alexander smiled at my tireless efforts but then turned serious. "Jagger's somewhere out here," he began, "hidden in a dark, secluded area or building big enough for two coffins," he said. When we reached the front doorstep, he went on,

"You understand, I'll have to search for them alone."

"Just because I jumped the fence tonight?"

"I can't risk putting you in danger again."

"But I can't spend the days *and* nights without you! And you need me—it's like Batman without Robin. I know all the creepy places to hide in this town."

"Well . . . you're right, but not quite—"

"Why not?"

"It's more like Gomez without Morticia," he said with a wink.

I leaned in to him and gave him a huge squeeze.

"We'll meet at sunset," he said, resigned. "And you can take me to one of those creepy places you are so fond of."

He gave me a lingering kiss, the kind that made my knees weak and my heart flutter like a hovering bat.

I unlocked the front door. "Till sunset," I said in a romantic daze and slowly turned to him.

Alexander had already vanished, just like any great vampire would.

I was sitting on my black beanbag chair recording the evening's events in my journal. I was too pre-occupied with thoughts of Luna and Jagger to sleep. I imagined the two of them flying through Dullsville's night sky together, looking down on Dullsvillians who would look like tiny nobodies as they got stuck in traffic, played golf, and dined in outdoor restaurants. I imagined the twins hiding in a basement-turned-dungeon, Jagger with pet tarantulas, and Luna dolled up in dresses made out of spiderwebs.

A scratching sound began outside my window. Nightmare jumped up on my computer desk and hissed at the darkness.

I raced to my window. "Alexander?" I called softly.

There were no signs of anything living or undead outside.

I closed the curtains and held an anxious Nightmare in my arms. There could have been a number of vampires lurking outside my window under the night sky. I just didn't know which one. I pondered placing a garlic clove on the win-dowsill, but I might repel the very vampire I wanted to attract.

4
Freaky Factory

The next evening I exclaimed, "I have great news!" as Alexander opened the Mansion door. He was sporting a black Alice Cooper T-shirt and oversized black pants riddled with safety pins. His dark eyes looked tired.

"What's wrong, sweetie?" I asked.

"Last night I searched all over town until I could feel the sun rise behind me," he began as we sat on the red-carpeted grand staircase. "I went to a vacant church and the abandoned farmhouse where we found Nightmare. I even found a dried-up well. The only thing in it was a broken bucket. I've been rattling my brain ever since and I didn't sleep all day.

"What's your good news?" he asked.

"Trevor is sick and will be absent from school all week. Plus that means he'll have to miss games and practices. It'll make it very hard for Jagger and Luna to take him to sacred ground if he's stuck inside."

Alexander's weary face came alive. "That's awesome! We'll have more time to find the Maxwells before they find him. But we have to do it quickly. The longer that Jagger and Luna wait for Trevor, the hungrier they will get. Literally."

"I spent all of algebra making a list of places they may be hiding out. It was hard. There aren't that many creepy places in this candy-colored town. I came up with ten—if you include my algebra class itself."

"Where's the list?" he asked eagerly.

"Well, Mr. Miller caught me writing in my notebook instead of figuring out what x plus y equaled and he confiscated my list."

"That's okay. I found a place I'd like to check out. But you have to promise me—"

"That I will love you forever? That's easy," I said, running my finger along one of the safety pins adorning his pants.

"Promise me you will stay out of trouble."

"That one is harder to commit to."

He leaned back. "Then you'll have to stay here."

"All right," I reconciled. "I'll behave."

"We won't be on sacred ground, so you'll be safe, but you need to stay close."

"Of course," I agreed. "Where are we going?"

"An abandoned factory at the edge of town."

"The Sinclair mill? That is totally dark, secluded, and big enough for a cemetery full of coffins."

Alexander borrowed his butler Jameson's Mercedes and we embarked on our own Magical Mystery Tour.

We left behind the twisty road of Benson Hill and headed past Dullsville High, through downtown, and finally over the railroad tracks into what the country clubbers called the "wrong" side of town.

"It's just up over there," I reminded him as I

pointed to a covered bridge.

We drove over the shaky bridge, around a winding, dark, fog-covered road, until the Mercedes's headlights shone upon a NO TRESPASSING sign on the gravel road leading to the vacant factory.

Spanning thirty-five acres, the Sinclair mill was surrounded by trees, overgrown bushes, and weeds. On the west side, a stagnant, murky creek barely rose during sporadic rainfalls. Fragrant wild flowers never seemed to mask its pungent smell.

The mill thrived in the 1940s, manufacturing uniforms for the war, employing hundreds of Dullsvillians. The once proudly puffing red-tiled S smokestack now stood silent. After the war the mill was bought by a linen company but ultimately couldn't compete with outsourcing, and the factory went bankrupt.

Now the Sinclair mill loomed over Dullsville like a listless monster. Half the factory's windows were blown out, and the others needed a gazillion liters of Windex. Police cars routinely patrolled the area, trying to deny graffiti artists a thirty-acre canvas.

Alexander parked the Mercedes next to several rusty garbage barrels. As soon as we stepped foot onto the grounds, we heard a barking off in the distance. We paused and glanced around. Maybe it was Jagger. Or maybe it was my own boyfriend's presence that was disturbing the dogs.

Supposedly, when the factory first opened, a fateful accident occurred when an elevator malfunctioned and plummeted to the basement, claiming several employees' lives. A rumor spread throughout Dullsville that on a full moon, a passerby could hear the mill workers' screams.

But the only ghosts I'd heard shrieking were actors covered in sheets when I was a child. We were visiting the factory for WXUV's Haunted House with my family.

"This was the haunted house's entrance," I recalled, heading for the broken metal door at the front of the mill. The words GET OUT WHILE YOU CAN! were still spray painted on the door from Halloweens past.

Alexander lit the way with his flashlight. I pulled the heavy door open and we crept inside.

A few spray paintings of humorous epitaphs

remained on the concrete walls.

Alexander and I cautiously walked over discarded boxes and headed for the main part of the factory. The twenty-five-thousand-square-foot room was empty of everything but dust. Round, discolored markings remained on the wooden floors where the machines had been bolted in place. Half the panes of glass were gone after decades of vandals, baseballs, and misguided birds.

"This room draws in too much daylight," Alexander said, looking at the missing windows. "Let's keep looking."

Alexander kindly held out his hand, like a Victorian gentleman, and with his flashlight led me down a dark two-flight staircase.

We passed through what must have been an employee locker room. The windowless room seemed ripe for a vampire to call home. Several metal lockers remained against the wall and even a few wooden benches. It now seemed like a dumping ground for garbage, littered with pop cans, bags, and a few discarded bicycle tires. No coffins were evident.

The basement was huge, cold, and damp.

Several mammoth-size furnaces filled the center of the room. I could almost hear the deafening roar of the once-burning kindling. Now the metal doors were rusty and unhinged, and a few were lying against the cement wall.

"Wow, with a few more spiderwebs and a couple of ghosts, this place would be perfect," I said.

"This could be ours," Alexander said, holding me close.

"We could put your easel over here," I said, pointing to an empty corner. "There would be plenty of room for you to paint."

"We could make shelves for your Hello Batty collection."

"And bring in a huge TV to watch scary movies. I wouldn't have to go to school and it could be dark twenty-four hours a day."

"No one would bother us, not even soccer snobs or vengeful vampires," Alexander said with a smile.

Just then we heard a barking sound.

"What was that?" I asked.

Alexander raised his eyebrow and listened. "We'd better go." He offered his hand and he led me out of the basement toward the front of the building.

In a small alcove Alexander found another staircase and lit our way back to the main floor.

While Alexander explored an office room, I investigated a hallway filled with boxes, a piece of cardboard covering a window, and a Stone Age freight elevator.

I removed the cardboard from the window to shed streetlight into the oversized lift.

The heavy metal elevator door hung partially open. I couldn't see clearly into it, so I snuck underneath the rusty door. When I stepped into the elevator, I heard a horrible screeching sound. I quickly turned around as the door slammed shut.

I stood in total darkness. I couldn't even see my own hands.

"Alexander! Let me out!" I called.

I banged my hands against the door.

"Alexander! I'm in the elevator!"

I felt along the side panel, vehemently trying to find a button to push. The surface was smooth. I fingered the adjacent wall and discovered what I thought might be a lever. I tried to pull it, but it didn't budge.

Normally I was comforted by darkness and found solace in tightly enclosed places. But now I was trapped.

My mind began to think of the poor souls who found their fate sealed in an elevator at the Sinclair mill.

I imagined bloody fingernails stuck to the inside door from decades of entombed young vandals.

I felt like I was going to be trapped forever.

I heard the cables rattling. Then heavy footsteps walked on the boards above me.

"Alexander! Get me out! Now!"

I wondered if the cables were still intact; if not, the elevator could plummet to the bowels of the basement at any moment.

I even thought I heard the screams of the ghosts—until I realized the screams were coming from me.

Suddenly the door pulled open, and I could barely see the oversized black pants and combat boots standing before me. My eyes squinted, trying to adjust to the moonlight that shined through the uncovered hallway window.

I was standing in the middle of an oval-shaped

ring of dirt, the front part messy, as if something heavy had dragged over it.

Alexander pulled me out before the door closed again.

I squeezed him with the little breath I still had in me.

"You saved my life."

"Hardly. But I think you found something."

We stood at a distance and examined the elevator's contents. Gravestone etchings covered the walls. In the corner sat an antique candelabra and a pewter goblet.

"Jagger had the same etchings at his Coffin Club apartment!" I said excitedly. "It's just missing the coffin."

"He must have left in a hurry."

"Why would he leave? Jagger could remain undiscovered for several eternities in this place. And this elevator could easily fit two coffins."

"He must have felt threatened."

"By the ghost story?"

"This old elevator isn't moving anywhere," Alexander reassured.

"Then what could possibly threaten Jagger?" I wondered.

While Alexander examined the elevator, I tried to catch my breath and combed the hallway for any more clues. Next to the boxes I noticed something silver catching the moonlight.

"What would this be doing here?" I asked, holding a garage door opener in my hand.

Alexander came over to me and examined my discovery.

At that moment, standing in the window right behind him, was a ghostly, attractive teen with white hair, the ends dyed bloodred. His eyes, one blue and one green, stared through me.

"Jagger!" I whispered.

"I know," Alexander answered, repeatedly clicking the opener in frustration. "He was here."

"No. He's here now! He's right outside!" I said, pointing to the window again.

Jagger flashed a wicked grin, his fangs gleaming.

Alexander quickly turned around, but Jagger had vanished.

"He was standing right there!" I cried, pointing to the window.

Alexander took off and I followed him back through the factory, past the ghostly Halloween props and out the front door.

When we reached the gravel drive, Alexander suddenly stopped next to the Mercedes.

He pressed the keys to the car in my hand and handed me the flashlight.

"Drive to the Mansion. I'll meet you there in half an hour," he said.

"But—"

"Please," he said, opening the door for me.

"Okay," I agreed, and reluctantly got inside.

Alexander closed the door. When I glanced back to say good-bye, he had vanished.

I locked the door and put the key in the ignition. As the crickets chirped and Alexander continued his search alone, I grew anxious. What if something happened to him? I couldn't hear his calls if I was miles away atop Benson Hill. I checked my container of garlic sealed safely inside my purse. I got out of the car and stuck the keys into my back pocket. I raced toward the east side of the factory with the flashlight in my hand.

The mill grounds had an eerie quietness to them. I felt as if someone were watching me. I looked up at the sky. I saw what appeared to be a bat hanging from the power lines above me. When I shined my light on the wire, it was gone.

I turned the corner of the factory to find Alexander pacing outside the hallway window.

"He was standing right here," I said.

"I should have known—," Alexander murmured.

"That I wouldn't stay in the car?"

Alexander shook his head and pointed toward the smokestack. Not twenty feet from where we were standing I could see plain as daylight what had threatened Jagger—a giant wrecking ball.

T hat night I sat in my computer chair, holding the garage door opener in my hand. I felt I held the key to cracking the Case of the Missing Twin Teen Vampires.

In fact, an empty garage was an awesome hiding place for a vampire. If a family were on vacation, they would have to drive the hour and a half to the nearest airport, therefore giving vacancy to a waiting coffin. With no one in the residence, Jagger and Luna could go undetected long enough to seduce Trevor into their vampirey lair.

If Alexander and I walked from garage door to garage door, it could take decades to discover which one Jagger and Luna were calling their latest batcave. By then Trevor would be "fluless" and return to practice in enough time for Luna to have sunk her fangs into him and the entire Dullsville High soccer team.

I hardly spoke to anyone in this town, much less knew the travel plans of the other Dullsvillians. I had to figure out a way to find out who was traveling, their destinations, and the durations of their stays. How could I get access to that information? Just then an idea struck me like a bolt of lightning. Of course I couldn't get the information—but I knew someone who could.

The next day, after school, Becky drove me to the Armstrong Travel Agency.

I missed the old girl. Since she'd begun dating Matt Wells and I'd met Alexander, we didn't have the endless free time to hang out, talk on the phone, or climb the Mansion's gates. So when we did have girl time, we made the most of it.

"I've heard rumors about that white-haired girl from Romania," she said when I got into her truck.

"What did you hear?" I asked, perking up after a long, mind-numbing school day.

"Well, that dude that was lurking at the drive-in when we saw *Kissing Coffins* was her brother."

"Yes . . . ," I began, hinting for more info.

"Matt says they've been asking around for Trevor. I think the dude wants to play on the soccer team, but he doesn't even go to our school."

"That's it?" I asked, disappointed. "I wouldn't worry about it. No one will take Matt's position away. Not even a vampire," I mumbled.

"What did you say?" she asked as she pulled the pickup in front of Armstrong Travel.

I stepped out of the truck.

"Are you sure you and Alexander aren't going to elope in Romania?" Becky teased.

"No, but if we do, I'll get *four* tickets."

I was happy to walk into Armstrong Travel in full goth garb—Herman Munster-size black boots, purple tights, and a black torn T-shirt dress—

instead of their Corporate Cathy dress code of tailored skirts and blouses.

I smiled at Ruby, who was seated at her desk, handing pamphlets to two customers. Ruby's friendly expression strained as I stood like an ill-mannered eyesore in the very conservative business.

"I'll be right with you," Ruby said, hinting at an out-of-the-way chair behind a rack of luggage tags.

"I'm just browsing," I said, and began glancing at a map of Hawaii.

Finally the young couple with Mexico brochures in their hands rose. They looked at me oddly, then cowered past, as if at any moment my bat body tattoo was going to jump off my arm and bite their heads off.

"I'll call you to confirm," Ruby said with a wave as the couple scurried out the door.

"Raven, it's great to see you," she greeted sincerely. "What brings you by?"

"Is Janice in?" I asked, secretly hoping she wasn't.

"No, she's at the post office. Is there something I can help you with?"

"Well . . . has anyone in town booked a

vacation in the last few days?"

"People book vacations every day. This *is* a travel agency, you know," she said with a smile.

"I mean—"

"Why would you want to know?"

Well, there are these two teen vampires who are hiding out in town, waiting for the right moment to bite Trevor Mitchell. I believe they are living in a vacant garage, probably belonging to a vacationer, I wanted to say. I imagined Ruby's pleasant face turning to shock, then horror, then her plugging away at her keyboard for a list of addresses. "You go, Raven Madison. Save Dullsville. Save the world."

"Uh . . . for a school report," I said instead. "I'm doing statistics on spring vacations."

"I'm sorry, hon, but I can't give out that information. You ought to know that; you worked here."

"But that's precisely the reason I thought you'd tell me."

"I'd love to help, but I just can't give out names, addresses, and itineraries," she said with a laugh. "In the wrong hands that information could be used for home invasions."

"Or at least garages," I said.

Ruby appeared confused just as the phone rang.

"Armstrong Travel, Ruby speaking. Can I help you make a reservation?" she said in an ultra-perky voice.

I fiddled with the white pens on her desk.

"Of course, let me see," she said, and began plugging away at her computer keyboard.

The phone rang again, this time lighting up line two of Ruby's white phone.

"Can I put you on hold?" Ruby asked. "Oh . . . you are calling from where?"

As the red light flashed and the phone continued to ring, I spun Ruby's lucite organizer and wondered how I could hack into their computer without the FBI finding out.

Ruby covered the receiver with her hand. "Do you mind answering that?" she asked, pointing to Janice's phone.

Who did she think I was? I didn't work here anymore, and I most certainly wasn't on the clock.

I went to Janice's desk, pressed line two, and picked up the phone. "Armstrong Travel, where Spain is hot and the men are hotter. Can I book you a trip there?"

"Do you have any specials on cruises?" a woman's voice asked.

"Janice?" I said. "Janice, is that you?"

Ruby glanced over at me.

"No, my name isn't Janice," the caller answered. "It's Liz. I'm interested in a vacation cruise to Alaska."

"Keys?" I asked loud enough for Ruby to hear. "You need car keys?"

"No," Liz corrected. "I said 'cruise.'"

Ruby looked over.

"You're at the post office? Your cell is breaking up. You need Ruby to pick you up?"

"I thought you said this was Armstrong Travel," Liz said.

"Let me talk," Ruby said to me. "Excuse me," she said politely to her caller, "I need to put you on hold."

"I'm sorry, I must have the wrong number," the inquiring Liz said, and hung up.

Ruby switched lines just as line two's red light went dead. "Janice? Janice?"

"Her cell kept dropping, then went dead. Maybe it wasn't her—"

"No, she's been frazzled all day."

Ruby hurried over to her business partner's desk and found a spare set of keys in her top drawer.

"Do you mind riding these over to the post office for me?"

This plan wasn't for *me* to leave. Ruby was making this difficult.

"I don't have my bike."

"Do you have your driver's license?"

"I have my temps."

Ruby glanced at me, then outside at her white Mercedes parked in front of the agency. I could see her mind race as she imagined me screeching down the street, blasting Marilyn Manson, and returning her car with newly painted black widow spiders running alongside the exterior.

"I'll have to close the agency," she said.

"Well . . . ," I began, twisting a lock of hair. "I could watch the office, if that would help you."

"You really aren't dressed appropriately," she said, eyeing my morose-looking outfit. "But I guess I don't have a choice. You wouldn't mind staying here for just a few minutes? I hate to close the agency."

"Well—"

"I won't be long, really," she said, gathering her purse and keys. "It would be a big help."

"Will I be paid the same rate as before?"

"Paid?" she asked with her hand on her hip. "I'll only be gone for a few minutes."

"How about throwing in a few plane tickets, too?"

Flustered, Ruby paused. "I'll give you ten dollars and a coupon for a free movie."

"Deal."

"You drive a hard bargain. That's what I've always liked about you," she said as she raced out the door.

I sat at Ruby's desk. I flipped through a *Condé Nast* magazine until I saw her get in her white Mercedes and drive off.

Now that I was employed again, even if only for twenty minutes, it was part of my job to be informed. I logged on to her computer using the same password I had when I was in her employ. Within moments I was surfing through the itineraries of vacationing Dullsvillians.

After my brief re-employment at Armstrong Travel, I arrived home, and geared up for my continuing mission. Wearing my Olivia Outcast backpack, I hopped on my mountain bike and headed for Loveland.

On the good side of the tracks sat Loveland, a quiet, middle-class community filled with vintage and modern homes.

I stopped at the corner of Shenandoah Avenue. I put on my sunglasses and Emily the Strange hoodie, so I wouldn't be recognized, though no one else in town dressed like I did. I pulled out my list of three Dullsvillian vacationers. For seven days and six nights, three Matten families—all related—were traveling to Los Angeles.

I felt like a gothic Goldilocks as I crept up the first driveway. The senior Matten Victorian-style house was gigantic. Their three-car garage could easily fit a few cars and a few sleeping vampires. I pressed the silver button and waited for the white door to open. It remained still.

A few houses down, the Mattens' eldest son's home appeared to be way too small. The one-car detached garage could barely fit a car, much less a coffin. I pressed the door opener anyway, but the door didn't budge.

Determined to find my nocturnal bounty, I made my way across the street, to the third Matten house. The Tudor-style home had a backyard garage hidden by a few trees. Their two-car garage seemed just right. Only it wasn't. The door didn't move.

Frustrated, I checked my list again.

By the time I headed for Oakley Village, I felt like I needed a few blood-filled amulets to recharge my pounding heart.

Oakley Village was a prosperous community of ultra-upscale homes. A who's who of successful Dullsvillians. I discovered on Ruby's computer that the Witherspoons, a retired couple who had just sold Witherspoon Lumber, were booked on a trip to Europe. They had departed three days ago and were scheduled to return in thirty days.

I rode up Tyler Street and turned into number 1455. The Witherspoons lived in a beautiful yellow-shuttered Victorian-style home with an attached three-car garage.

I quickly snuck up their driveway.

I checked out my surroundings to make sure there weren't any nosy neighbors eyeballing me. When I saw I was in the clear, I aimed the opener at the door. I took a deep breath and pressed the silver button.

The door didn't move. I pressed it again.

Nothing happened. This couldn't be!

I tapped it over and over. Still, the door remained fixed.

I ran to the front of the house and pressed my face against the carport's yellow-shuttered window. The garage was empty of cars *and* coffins.

I stormed down the driveway to retrieve my bike and checked my Hello Batty watch. I had only a few more hours left of sunlight until this hunter would become the hunted.

I held the door opener in my hand. Which garage did it belong to?

Frustrated, I decided to return home, wait until sunset for Alexander to awake, then confess I hadn't made any Underworldly discoveries. I coasted down the winding road, heading for a shortcut through the Oakley Woods.

I began riding over the bumpy terrain, but then I saw something odd. Sticking out from behind a large pile of wood chips was a vintage hearse!

I pulled my bike up alongside the ghastly car. The circa 1970s Cadillac midnight mobile was beautiful; it had a sleek, long black hood with a silver bat ornament, white-walled tires, a black carriage adorned with a chrome S-shaped insignia, and black curtains. On the left rear quarter panel was a decal of a white skull and cross-bones.

I hopped off my bike and peered into the driver's seat, where I could see restored shiny black vinyl upholstered seats and a tiny white skeleton hanging from the rearview mirror.

I tried to peer in the back window, but the curtains were drawn. The license plate's county sticker was from Hipsterville—the town a few hundred miles away from Dullsville where the Coffin Club was and where I first encountered the nefarious Jagger. The license plate read: I BITE.

"What are you doing here?" a familiar voice asked.

I nearly jumped out of my boots.

I turned around to find Billy Boy and Henry standing right in front of me.

"I told you it was for real," Henry proudly proclaimed.

"Wow. It is freaky," Billy Boy remarked. "But why is it parked in the woods?"

"I don't know. I discovered it yesterday on my way home from math club," Henry replied.

"Is there a body inside?" Billy Boy asked, nervously trying to peer into the back window.

"No. But I think we could arrange that," I said.

Billy Boy backed away from the macabre mobile.

"Have you seen anyone driving it?" I inquired.

Henry shook his head.

"You still haven't told me why you are out here," Billy Boy charged.

I fingered the garage door opener in my hand. And then it hit me.

There was only one person I knew in Dullsville who could help me whittle down my search—one person who could figure out how to use a garage door opener to unlock his locker or even unbolt his bedroom door. And his five-foot-two-inch nerd body was standing right in front of me.

"I found this," I said, showing Henry. "I'm sure the person who lost it would like to get their car out—or back in."

"You want to know which door it is so you can break in," Billy Boy alleged.

"I wouldn't be breaking in if I had the opener, now would I?" I snarled. "Besides, I'm not a thief. It's my civic duty to return it to its rightful owner."

"Let's see it," Henry said like a jeweler inspecting a precious stone. "This is an Aladdin.

I'd say one out of ten homes use this manufacturer. It's the same kind we use."

"You do?" I asked curiously.

"Yes. And this one looks familiar."

"You've seen it? Can you tell me which homes might use them?"

"I was missing one the other day," he said, wrinkling his face in thought. "Hey—"

Henry lived in a five-bedroom Colonial-style house just up the road. I'd visited his house once before, when Becky and I were in need of accessories for our *Kissing Coffins* outfits. Henry supplied us with fangs, blood pellets, and scars.

I imagined bloodthirsty vampire twins anxiously waiting in coffins in his family's garage as he innocently played with fake blood and fangs above them in his bedroom.

"This couldn't be it," I said protectively, and immediately grabbed back the opener.

"But I swore—"

"Are your parents home?" I asked.

"No, they went to San Diego for a medical convention."

My heart stopped pulsing. "Did they plan their trips through Armstrong Travel?" I asked.

"They booked their tickets online," he answered, confused.

"Then who is home with you?"

"Our housekeeper, Nina," he continued.

"Do you want Raven to be your babysitter?" Billy Boy teased.

Then my thoughts turned serious. Behind that mechanical shield of wood might lie two sleeping teen vampires.

"I'll walk you to your house," I said. "You can never be too careful these days."

I followed the two nerds up the steep road to Henry's house. When we reached his driveway I saw the three-car garage attached to his home. And then, a few yards back, sat another two-car detached garage.

One garage wasn't good enough? I thought as we approached Henry's house.

"I'll tell Mom you are doing your homework *inside* Henry's," I said. "You should stay indoors today trading your Pokémon cards or whatever it is you do. It's supposed to rain."

"I told you she's weird," Billy Boy whispered as the two went inside.

I waited for a moment, walked my bike

halfway down the driveway, then quietly doubled back.

I rested my bike against the side of his brick house.

Since Henry was staying with Nina, I assumed the attached garage, with the comings and goings of a preteen and a hardworking housekeeper, was too exposed for a hiding vampire. But I peered into it anyway. I saw a vintage Rolls and shelves of tools.

Now that Henry and Billy Boy were safely inside the house finding square roots, I ran to the detached garage. I took a deep breath and aimed the door opener.

I pressed the silver button.

Nothing happened. The door didn't budge. The opener didn't click.

I pressed it again.

The door remained still.

"It's not for that," Henry said as he and Billy Boy came out of the house.

I jumped back.

"I open it this way," Henry said, and stepped on a WELCOME HOME mat.

The garage door began to open.

"No! Cover your eyes!" I cried, and put my hand out in front of them as if my lanky arm could block them from seeing two coffins.

It was too late.

The garage door slowly opened like a creaky coffin lid. My heart stopped beating. I could barely open my eyes.

Then I saw them. Not one but two silver BMWs, both emblazoned with red Dullsville Middle School "I'm the proud parent of an honor student" bumper stickers.

I went inside the garage and looked around, underneath, and inside the back of the luxury vehicles.

"What is wrong with you?" Billy asked. "You're not used to cars without skulls and cross-bones?"

"Well, if this doesn't open the garage," I argued, now fatigued and angry, "what does it do?"

We followed Henry into his gigantic back-yard, which was the size of a football field, com-plete with a mosaic-tiled patio, an Olympic-size pool, and a million-dollar flower garden.

He aimed the opener toward the house and pressed the button. Suddenly floodlights, scattered around his property, illuminated the already sunlit backyard.

"Nina gets freaked out when she house-sits," Henry stated. "She claims she sees shadows and things moving in the backyard. I keep the lights on when my parents are out of town. But since I lost it, it's been pitch-black back here."

I didn't understand. What did this have to do with Jagger? Why was he returning for it? Or was he making sure it was still there?

I walked past Henry's pool and garden and into his backyard to see what he needed to illuminate. The huge field was wasted on a boy who was more interested in throwing around scientific theories than footballs.

Then I saw it. In the far corner of the yard— at least sixty yards from where we stood—was an A-framed treehouse.

"That is perfect!" I exclaimed.

"I used to spend a lot of time out here until my dad built me a lab in the basement—now I'm down there more," Henry said. "He just bought me a telescope to entice me outdoors and into the treehouse again, but it's still in the box in my room."

"Yeah, it's been forever since we've been up here," Billy Boy added.

"What's that?" I asked, pointing to a rope with a rusty pulley dangling from one of the massive branches.

"It's a principle similar to one used in canal houses in Europe," Henry said behind me. "I had it installed to lift up furniture."

Or coffins? I wondered.

"Want to take a look?" he asked proudly.

I still had the protection of the sun's rays and the unyielding curiosity of a cat, but if I rode to the Mansion and waited for Alexander to wake up, then Jagger and Luna would be rising, too. The moon was ticking. My heart was pounding. First I had to make sure Henry and Billy Boy were far away from the treehouse.

"How about putting together that telescope your dad bought you?" I suggested.

Henry's face lit up as if I'd just invited him to see a private screening of *Lord of the Rings*. "I didn't know you were into astronomy," he said.

Billy Boy looked at me skeptically. "She probably just wants to look in your neighbor's windows."

I glared at my brother.

"And we'll need maps of the constellations," I added. "And don't forget charts and any diagrams you might have."

"There are quite a few constellations you can see in the daylight."

"We'll be able to see more clearly when the sun sets. So take your time. Don't come out here until you have everything ready. I'll wait here."

As soon as the two nerd-mates reached the back patio, I started to climb the thick wooden ladder that led up the tree, the boards creaking underneath my combat boots.

I stepped onto the uneven treehouse deck.

The wooden door slowly creaked open.

If Jagger and Luna were hiding here, then I realized why Jagger left the door opener at the factory. If Henry continued to use it to illuminate the treehouse, Jagger and Luna risked being discovered and scorched by the light.

When I opened the wooden door, I expected to find the coffins I had been searching for.

Instead I saw a run-down 3-D version of *Dexter's Laboratory*. On a folding lab table sat dusty beakers, petri dishes, and a microscope.

The periodic table and a photosynthesis chart were taped to the slanting walls.

The treehouse interior was divided by a black curtain. I slowly pulled it back.

What I found took my breath away. Hidden in the shadows of the sloping wooden wall was a black coffin adorned with gothic band stickers, encircled in dirt. And resting next to it was a pale pink coffin!

I'd dreamed about a moment like this all my vampire-obsessed life, never to believe it would actually come to fruition. This was my chance to witness up close and personal a modern-day Nosferatu in his natural habitat. And with Luna, the moment was even more meaningful, because she, once human, was now a vampiress. I was looking firsthand into a world that I'd always envisioned being part of.

I crept toward the pink casket, hoping for a peek at what it was like inside. It was as fashionable as it was spooky. The once mortal Luna was now living in the Underworld next to her twin brother. I wondered if she regretted her decision.

I tiptoed over to Jagger's coffin. I gently touched the wooden top with the tip of my fingers. I held my breath and pressed my ear to the lid. I could hear the faint breathing of someone who was in a heavy stage of sleep. And then I heard him stir.

"Raven!" yelled Billy Boy.

I jumped back.

"Where are you?" he shouted.

I raced out of the room and promptly closed the curtain.

Billy Boy, with rolled-up maps under one arm, was fiddling with the microscope. "If you think this place is cool, you should see his basement."

"I've seen enough petri dishes to last me a lifetime. Let's go." I pulled my brother by the sleeve of his striped Izod T-shirt and led him to the treehouse door.

Even though I had daylight protecting me, I glanced back, expecting Luna and Jagger to somehow be following me.

We reached the bottom of the creaky ladder to find Henry carrying the telescope.

"Let's take this over to our place," I said, grabbing the telescope. "This treehouse isn't up to code."

"But my dad just—"

"Speaking of your dad, I think you should stay at our house for the week," I said to Henry.

My brother and his nerd-mate's eyes perked up.

"Seriously. You shouldn't be in this huge house without your parents. And I'm sure Nina could use a vacation."

"That'll be awesome. Your parents won't mind?" Henry asked politely.

"Pack your briefcase, and not another word," I ordered as we headed for his house.

Shortly after dusk I put on my Emily the Strange sweatshirt hoodie and secured Henry's garage door opener safely inside the pouch pocket. I raced to the Mansion and tore up the broken cement stairs to the front door and anxiously rapped the serpent knocker.

Alexander opened the door. I was greeted by my handsome boyfriend, standing in a black-and-white bowling shirt and black jeans with hanging silver chains, wearing a smile that could melt any sixteen-year-old vampire-obsessed goth. Before he even had a chance to say hello, I blurted out, "I've got major news. I've found the coffins!"

"That's awesome! Where?"

"I'll show you," I said, grabbing his hand and leading him out of the Mansion and toward the Mercedes.

Alexander drove me to the edge of the Oakley Woods, and we hopped out of the car. "Jagger's hearse was right here," I said, pointing to a pile of wood chips.

We followed fresh tire marks leading out of the woods, which turned into muddy tracks heading up the street.

"They must have left in the hearse. If we move quickly, we can remove the coffins."

Alexander parked the Mercedes outside Henry's house and we crept through the backyard.

"There it is," I said proudly, pointing to the treehouse.

Alexander and I watched for any signs that Jagger and Luna might still be inside. There were no candles flickering, or movement from the white-curtained windows.

"This is the pulley Henry used to hoist his

furniture into the treehouse," I whispered, holding the dangling rope. "Jagger must have used it, too. This is how we'll get the caskets down."

"Stay here," Alexander said. "If you see anything, don't hesitate to take off. I can handle myself."

I glanced around. "But—"

When I turned back, Alexander was gone.

Once again Alexander was protecting me. Didn't he know we could move the coffins quicker if we both helped? I searched around the tree and found no signs of Luna or Jagger.

I tiptoed up the ladder and entered the tree-house.

"What are you doing up here?" Alexander asked. "I thought we had an agreement."

"We did. But I missed you," I said, giving him a quick hug. "Besides, I've been up here before and I can show you around."

Alexander shook his head, went to the window, and peered out.

"We don't have much time," he said. "Where are they hiding? In the petri dishes?"

"No, silly." I pulled the black curtain open.

The darkened room was different from what

I'd seen a few hours earlier—the coffin lids were open!

I peeked into Luna's casket. It held a neatly made pink satin comforter with a black lace border, a pink faux fur pillow, and a black Scare Bear plush.

The gravestone etchings Alexander and I had seen at the linen factory lining the rustic elevator were now tacked up to the slanting treehouse walls. The antique candelabra and pewter goblet Jagger had used at Dullsville's cemetery during his attempted covenant ceremony were resting on the floor. A black duffel bag and a Little Nancy Nightmare backpack were shoved in the corner. Next to them was an open box from the Coffin Club, loaded with blood-filled amulets from the mortal clubsters—the only way for the pair to survive without drawing attention or blood from Dullsville's mortals. Then I noticed a blood-red party-size cooler. I knelt beside it and fingered the edge of the white Styrofoam lid. What was being chilled inside? Packets or bottles of blood? Transplanted organs? A human head? I took a breath and began to lift the lid.

"Raven!" Alexander said.

I almost jumped out of my own pale skin.

"I need you to hold the door open for me," Alexander whispered. "I'll have to drag the coffins through."

"Let me help you," I offered.

"I'll do it," he said, always the gentleman. "I don't want you to hurt yourself."

Alexander started to close Jagger's coffin lid when we heard voices coming from outside.

"That might be Henry and Billy Boy," I said. "We can't let them up here."

"Stay here. I'll divert them."

I hid in the shadows and, naturally curious, began to further search the teen vampires' hideout. A plastic end table was turned into a goth makeup counter. I examined Luna's neatly arranged pink and black eye shadows, gray lipsticks, and mud-colored glosses. I opened a small bottle of Cotton Candy nail polish.

"So how do you like being a vampire?"

I dropped the nail polish and quickly turned around.

Jagger, wearing a white "Bite Me, I'm Transylvanian" T-shirt and black army fatigues, was standing before me.

"What are you doing here?" I questioned.

"Shouldn't I be asking you that?" he asked. His white hair hung in his face.

"I was just leaving—"

"I thought you'd be happy to see me. After all, haven't you been spending the last few days searching for *me*?"

I stepped back and looked away from his blue and green hypnotic eyes. I didn't want to return to Dullsville's cemetery with him again.

"Luna claimed she saw you reflected in the Fun House's Hall of Mirrors," he said, walking closer.

I paused. I could barely breathe. I looked at the white-curtained window, planning to make my escape.

"But I knew better," he continued. "You might fool her with those circus mirrors, but not me. I saw Alexander bite you and transform you right in front of my eyes. I regretted the day I didn't get to you first."

I breathed again. But only for a moment as he inched toward me.

"Isn't Sterling fulfilling your darkest needs?" he whispered. "I thought you got what you wanted."

"I did."

"Then you wouldn't be here, now would you? Sterling's not cut out for what you really desire, is he? That's why you are trying to find me."

I paused. I stepped past him, but he grabbed my hand.

He lifted it. "You have very long love veins," he said, running his finger along a skinny horizontal blue vein, his black painted fingernail in sharp contrast to my pasty skin. "See here, how it splinters off? As if you were pursuing a path with one love, but then you chose another."

"I used to be crazy about Marilyn Manson. Now I love Alexander," I said sharply.

He held my hand tighter. "We are the same now, you and I."

"We never were, nor will we ever be, the same," I argued.

Jagger didn't seem convinced.

"How about we share a drink together?" he asked, lifting my wrist to his mouth. "Then we will be closer than ever."

I quickly jerked my arm away. "Alexander quenches any thirst I have."

"Is it everything you thought it would be?

Being a princess of the night?"

"Why don't you ask Luna."

Then it hit me: If Jagger was here, where was his twin sister?

I raced past him, out to the deck of the treehouse, and looked out to the yard. Alexander was searching the poolside grounds.

A few yards from the treehouse, I thought I saw some long white hair poking out from behind one of the trees.

I turned around, expecting to find Jagger mischievously grinning. But he was no longer standing behind me.

Instead I saw Jagger and Luna darting from underneath the treehouse, through the backyard, toward my unsuspecting boyfriend.

"Alexander!" I called.

I was too far away to reach Alexander before they did. And what could I do against two real vampires, anyway? How could a mortal goth stop them?

Then I remembered. "Alexander—cover yourself! With a towel! Now!" I shouted.

He looked confused but snatched a folded beach towel from a lounge chair, crouched down, and enveloped himself with it.

I pulled my hoodie over my head and drew the strings tightly shut.

I grabbed the garage door opener from my pocket and pointed it at Henry's house.

I took a deep breath and pressed my finger on the silver button as hard as I could.

The lights burst on, illuminating the entire backyard, including Jagger and Luna.

The two vampires stopped dead in their tracks. The sudden burst of bright light was like kryptonite. They shielded their pale faces with their skinny bleach white arms. They each hissed and fled into the darkness.

I flew down the ladder and raced to the pool deck. Breathless, I finally reached Alexander, still covered, on a lounge chair.

I aimed the garage door opener at the house again, pressed the silver button, and the once-illuminated backyard turned black.

It took a moment for my eyes to adjust to the darkness. I could see Alexander, his hair tousled, a towel by his side.

"Quick thinking," he complimented, and gave me a long kiss.

"We better get out of here—," I said.

"Jagger will be more determined than ever to get Trevor now that he knows we've found his hideout. They won't wait much longer."

8

Gossip and Garlic

I f there ever was a morning I didn't want to get out of bed, this was it. After pressing the snooze bar repeatedly, I unplugged my *Nightmare Before Christmas* alarm clock and stashed it under my bed.

What I couldn't unplug was my mother's voice.

"Raven!" she called for the millionth time from downstairs. "You've overslept. Again."

After a quick shower, I threw on a black-on-black ensemble. I dragged myself into the kitchen to gulp down some of the leftover morning

113

sludge that Dad called "coffee."

I found Billy Boy already commandeering the chair by the TV with our new house guest, Henry. The nerd-mates were glued to the screen, watching historic footage of battleships blasting their cannons and devouring Pop-Tarts and Crunch Berries.

With every crunch of the captain and boom of a cannon, I felt like my head was behind enemy lines.

"Turn that off!" I whined, and switched the channel to the Home Shopping Network.

A petite blond with a perfect french manicure was modeling bedazzling silver bracelets.

"Hurry, there's only fifty seconds left!" I warned Billy Boy. "You could own one in just five easy payments. The blue topaz matches your eyes."

Billy Boy raced to the TV and wrangled the control out of my hand. "Get off!" he said, switching it back to the History Channel. "If you'd watch, maybe you'd learn something. Then your report card could be framed in Dad's office, instead of ending up in his paper shredder."

I stirred cream and a pound of sugar into a

java-filled Dullsville Country Club mug and poured myself a small bowl of Count Chocula. The gun battle and excessive crunching continued. I could barely open my charcoal eyelids wide enough to see the chocolate vampires floating in the milk among the marshmallow ghosts and bats.

My mom burst into the kitchen in her Corporate Cathy gear—a crisp gray DKNY pantsuit and Kate Spade mules—and opened the fridge door. "Morning," she said gleefully. "I thought you'd never get up."

"I didn't either," I grumbled.

"I saw Mrs. Mitchell at the pharmacy last night buying Trevor some cough syrup," she said, placing her Tupperware bowl filled with low-fat, low-taste premade salad in her Bloomingdale's tote bag. "Trevor must have the same cold you had."

"Yeah, he's been out of school. It's been the first time I only detested school instead of hating it."

"Well, I think he's on the mend. His mother told me a girl has been bringing him protein shakes and he's feeling better."

"You mean one of the cheerleaders, right?" I queried.

"No. Mrs. Mitchell made it very clear this girl is new to town and dresses—well, not very conservatively," my mom said, grabbing a bottled water and closing the fridge door.

"You mean, like me?"

My mother paused.

It was Luna.

"Is it the white-haired girl Trevor was with at the Spring Carnival?" Billy Boy asked.

"It may be," my mom answered. "I didn't see them together."

"I just saw her from a distance," my brother said. "But a kid at Math Club swears she has a twin. They were spotted coming out of the cemetery. Her brother was dressed like he just stepped off a pirate ship.

"Kids are saying they sleep in sewers," Billy Boy continued.

"It's not nice to gossip," my mother warned.

"I heard they're ghosts. One dude claims you can see right through them," Henry said.

"And talk about tattoos and piercing," Billy Boy added, "I heard he has more holes in his head than you," Billy Boy said to me.

"I have tattoos," I said, rolling up my sleeve and showing him a bat tattoo.

"Your dad told you to wash that off," my mother advised.

"And he has pierced kneecaps," my brother went on.

"Well, I'll pierce your kneecaps if you don't stop gossiping like two old ladies."

"All right. Boys, you are going to miss your bus if you don't finish soon," my mother ordered.

Henry and Billy Boy placed their empty bowls in the dishwasher.

"Mom, did Mrs. Mitchell say this girl brought Trevor protein shakes?" I asked.

"Supposedly they are special shakes from Romania. I asked Mrs. Mitchell to get the recipe for me."

Delicious drink, I thought. *Ingredients: One cup crushed ice. One banana. One vial vampire's blood.*

"I don't think you'd like this particular Romanian drink."

Finally we got a reprieve from the gunfire, and a commercial for Garlic One gelcaps came on the TV. Billy Boy aimed the remote to switch it off.

"No, wait," I said.

"You're suddenly interested in history?" Billy Boy asked proudly. "Maybe I'm rubbing off on you after all."

"Shh . . ."

My mom followed Billy Boy and Henry as they headed for the front door.

"Garlic One," the commercial continued. "Natural and odorless. Helps promote cardio-vascular health with just one capsule a day."

Their slogan should say, "An odor-free way to keep the vampires away."

I was struck with an idea. Why hadn't I thought of it sooner? There was nothing I loved more than a brand-new plan!

Hey, Beck, do you mind stopping at Paxx Pharmacy?" I asked my best friend when I hopped into her pickup. "I just have to buy a few things on the way to school."

"But Matt will be waiting by the bleachers for us. I don't want to be late."

"It'll only take a sec," I pleaded.

The old girl was as hot-glued to her soccer sweetheart as I was to my vampire boyfriend. I would have been sickened if I didn't understand her amorous devotion.

"Okay," she finally agreed. "I could get Matt

some candy. He loves red licorice."

I remember when Becky and I would hang outside Paxx's and eat twines of red licorice until we felt ill. Now, instead of creating new memories with me, she was creating them with Matt.

I turned to my best friend, who was wearing khakis and a pale blue button-down shirt. As long as I'd known Becky, she'd worn jeans and an oversized sweater. How long had I not noticed the change?

"Besides, it will give us a chance to hang out," she added kindly.

Becky was right. I'd been so wrapped up in diverting the union between Trevor and Luna that I hadn't any time left to talk, or even open my eyes!

Now that we had beaus, we didn't cling to each other like we had before. Did that mean we didn't need each other at all?

"It's been forever since we've had girl time," I agreed.

"I know, it's great we have boyfriends, but I'm missing our friendship."

"Me too!" I said. "We have to make time for us."

"It's a pact," she said, extending her pinky finger.

"A pact," I said, entwining my own in hers.

More than spending time apart, I felt like I was in the dark alone, not being able to share with my best friend the fact that our town was crawling with vampires.

"If I tell you something, can you promise not to tell anyone? Not even Matt?" I asked.

"Is it about sex?"

"No. It's even more top secret."

"What's more top secret than sex?"

I was ready to spill my guts. To tell my best friend why my boyfriend was never seen in daylight. To explain to her why Jagger drove a hearse. Why the ghostlike Luna had suddenly come to Dullsville.

But Becky's cherub face looked so happy, her biggest concern being what new outfit to wear to school, what brand of candy treat to buy for Matt. I couldn't spoil her perfect world.

"We're having a pop quiz in Shank's class tomorrow."

"Duh," she said, rolling her eyes. "Everyone knows that."

"Really?" I asked, almost horrified. "Maybe I'm losing my touch."

I was hunkered down in the vitamin-and-herb aisle, studying Mother Nature's remedies and filling my red plastic shopping basket with vitamin C and boxes of Garlic One gelcaps, when Becky finally caught up to me.

"I thought you were feeling better," she said, holding several packages of red licorice.

"I am, but I want to stock up."

"Garlic tablets?" she asked, confused. "I thought you were over your vampire obsession now that you are dating Alexander."

"I am. I just saw this commercial—"

"Speaking of Alexander," she interrupted excitedly, "would you two want to meet up at Hatsy's Diner after the soccer game tonight?"

How could I tell my best friend no after we'd just made a pinky-swear pact to hang out more? As long as I was with Alexander and Trevor was home sick, I reasoned, we were all safe.

"Yes, that's a great idea. I don't think Alexander's ever been to Hatsy's."

Becky and I brought our purchases to the

counter. We stood, unnoticed, as an elderly clerk hid behind a tabloid mag and her teenage clerkmate filed packets of developed prints.

"Those two kids I was telling you about were in here last night," the elderly clerk gossiped. "I think they are cousins of that weird mansion family on Benson Hill."

"I heard they look like walking corpses," the younger one chimed back.

"They do. I just don't get why kids today think it's cool to look like they've just come out of a coffin."

"I've heard one of them drives a hearse."

Just then the elderly clerk put down her paper and spotted me. Her eyes bugged out like she'd seen a ghost.

"I'm sorry," she apologized. "Have you been waiting long?"

"An eternity!" I said.

So Jagger and Luna were beginning to make their presence known throughout Dullsville. Were they bored, careless, or marking their territory?

Even though Trevor and I'd spent our lives at each other's throats, I didn't want Luna and

Jagger after his. Besides they were looking to do far more damage than wringing his neck. A mixture of emotions flooded through me—protecting a fellow Dullsvillian from a deadly duo, thwarting a plan to have a nefarious soccer snob wreaking havoc, and diverting a plot to have my nemesis turned into a vampire before I was.

I'd have to get these tablets to Trevor. At any moment, Jagger or Luna could strike—or in their case, bite.

Though keeping up my new vampire identity was exhausting, I was really beginning to enjoy it. Everything I felt before as a vampire-obsessed goth I now had to live out—my distaste for the light and passion for darkness, having a secret identity, and being an insider instead of an outsider. I imagined the rest—flying high in Dullsville's sky, living in a spooky dungeon, Alexander and I cuddling the day away in a king-size coffin.

As the sun began to set, I rode my bike to Trevor's, with my Paxx Pharmacy bag safely inside my Olivia Outcast backpack. I'd already called Jameson and told him I'd be a few minutes late to meet Alexander. It was crucial that I keep up my vampire charade and wait until darkness until I visited Trevor, just in case Trevor spilled my visit to Luna. If he shared with her that I'd visited him after school the first day he was sick, Luna could assume Trevor was delirious from his cold medicine. But now that my nemesis was on the mend, I had to cover my tracks. I couldn't give them any reason to suspect I was still a mortal.

"I've been waiting all day for you," Trevor said as he opened the front door. He was wearing plaid flannel pajama pants and a long-sleeve Big Ten surf shirt and was sporting a much healthier glow—a bad sign he'd be coming back to school, but a good sign he hadn't been bitten.

"You missed me?" I asked with a saccharine grin.

"I thought you were Luna," he said, disappointed. "We're not buying Ghoul Scout cookies today," he said, closing the door.

I quickly blocked the door with my boot.

"I'm putting the final touches on my health project," I said, opening the door and stepping inside.

"Do you want me to feel better or put me in the morgue?"

"Do I have a choice?"

"Why don't you write down in your report the reason for Trevor Mitchell's illness. Two words: Raven Madison. I'm sure the Infectious Disease Institute has heard of you," Trevor said.

I ignored his rude comments and walked into his newly painted sunflower yellow kitchen, which still smelled like fresh paint.

"I've heard you've been getting visits from a ghostly candy stripper. I mean, striper," I said with a grin.

"Sounds like someone is jealous."

I pulled out my Paxx Pharmacy bag and placed it on the granite-top kitchen island.

"My mom already got me medicine."

"It's just a few things so I can get extra credit. Vitamin C, a bag of cough drops, and Garlic One capsules."

"Garlic capsules? I'll smell like an Italian restaurant."

"They're good for cardiovascular health. Should help you on the soccer field."

"Didn't you see all my trophies? I can play in

my sleep," he said arrogantly.

I was running out of options, and time. I had to go for the jugular.

"Word on the street is, these are a major aphrodisiac. Gives off a scent that girls find irresistible. Something about pheromones. Anyway, someone like you shouldn't need it," I said, heading for the front door with the capsules.

"Hey, wait," he said, catching up to me in the entranceway. "Leave those here." He grabbed the package from my hand. "Not for me, of course. For the guys on the team."

One block north of Dullsville's downtown square sat Hatsy's Diner—a quaint fifties restaurant complete with teal blue and white vinyl booths, a black-and-white-checked tile floor, neon Coke signs, and a menu of cheeseburgers, atomic fries, and the thickest chocolate shakes in town. The waitresses donned red diner uniforms while the waiters dressed as soda jerks. Occasionally Becky and I would frequent Hatsy's after school when we managed to scrounge enough change to cover an order of onion rings and a mediocre tip.

Alexander and I arrived at Hatsy's. A few families and young couples were scattered around the diner. The soccer players were already gulping down malts and fries at two large tables. All eyes turned to us as we walked through the clean, crisp, bright diner in our usual blackness.

A surge of excitement shot through me—I felt like a gothic princess on the arm of her handsome gothic prince, although I knew the stares were from ridicule rather than envy.

Alexander studied the framed Bobby Darrin, Ricky Nelson, and Sandra Dee records, too engrossed in his new surroundings to feel self-conscious.

Matt and Becky were sitting alone in a corner booth.

"Hey, guys, we're over here," Becky called.

Alexander and I nestled into the booth.

"I thought you'd be sitting with the rest of the soccer team," I remarked as we grabbed the menus resting behind the chrome napkin holder.

"We thought it might be cozier if it were just us," Becky said.

A tall waitress with an hourglass figure, a brunette beehive, and white cat's-eye glasses approached our table, chomping on a wad of pink bubble gum.

"Hi, my name is Dixie," she said, cracking her gum. She pulled out an order pad from her white apron. "What can I get you?"

"Two vanilla shakes and an order of atomic fries," Matt said.

"And we'd like the same, but make the shakes chocolate, please," Alexander said.

Dixie blew a big bubble and popped it with her front teeth.

Then she sashayed off toward the kitchen. All the guys in the diner gawked at her, even Alexander and Matt.

"When I grow up, I want to look just like that," I said to Alexander.

"You already do," he said, putting his arm around me and giving me a squeeze.

Alexander's eyes lit up as he spotted the vintage tabletop jukebox. "This is cool," he said, flipping through the menu of fifties tunes. "I've only seen these in movies."

I'd forgotten that my boyfriend spent so much of his life hidden away in his attic room, far from the mundane musings of mortals. I got goose bumps seeing him so fascinated in his new surroundings as he examined the list of titles and artists.

"Elvis rocks," he said, elated.

I dug my hand into my purse and placed a quarter in the jukebox.

A moment later, "Love Me Tender" played over the speakers.

Alexander smiled a sweet smile and squeezed my hand. His leg was touching mine, and I could feel him tapping his combat boots to the beat of the song underneath the table.

"So what have you guys been up to lately?" Matt asked.

"Hunting for coffins," Alexander said.

Becky and Matt looked at us oddly.

"The usual," I said, smiling.

Matt and Becky laughed.

"So how was your game?" Alexander asked Matt as he put his napkin on his lap.

"We kicked butt. But only because Trevor played."

"No," Becky defended. "You scored, too."

"I thought he was sick," I said.

"Well, he managed to show up and score a

few goals. As much as I hate to say it, we're not a winning team without him."

"Did he go home?" I asked.

"No, he's over there," Matt said, pointing behind me.

I turned around. Trevor was in the far end of the diner, playing pinball.

"He shouldn't be out at night," I declared.

Becky looked perplexed.

"I'm using him as my project for health class. The night air isn't good for a cold. Excuse me, I'll be back in a sec," I said, awkwardly scooting out of the booth.

I could feel eyeballs on me as I walked across the diner, but not for the same reason they had been looking at Dixie.

I tapped on Trevor's shoulder. "What are you doing here?"

My nemesis glanced at me and rolled his eyes. "Looks like I'm playing pinball."

"You're sick. You shouldn't be out where you can pick up more germs."

"Believe me, with you standing next to me, I've already picked up several diseases," he said, pressing the flippers with gusto.

"You should be at home," I ordered.

The ball hit a bumper, causing the game board to light up. "You left Monster Boy to talk to me?" he asked. "You've been to my house twice. I'm beginning to think—"

"It's best you don't think. Did you take your garlic?"

"I had a game, not a date," he said, tilting the machine.

"You should be resting."

"You sound like my mother," he said, banging on the flippers.

"Well, maybe you should listen to her." ᐧ

"Why, so she can tell me not to see Luna? Has my mom been talking to you?"

"She doesn't approve?" I asked, curious.

"What do you think?"

"Your mother is right this time. Luna isn't your type. You need a girl with a tiara, not a tattoo."

"But do I really? Luna dresses like you and you've been trying to convince me for years that you are not a mutant. Did you ever think it wasn't your clothes that led people to think you were a freak?"

"So what do you see in her?" I interrogated.

"She's the new girl, beautiful and mysterious. Kind of what you liked in Alexander."

"That's completely different. I like Alexander because he is unlike anyone I've ever met and exactly like me. But Luna isn't your type. She's too goth."

"Just like someone we know . . ."

"You'd risk your popularity for her?" I whispered with a twinge of jealousy.

I hated to admit it, but deep down I did wonder what Trevor saw in Luna that he didn't see in me.

"Are you kidding? I'll be even more popular for scoring the *new* goth girl rather than the *old* one."

It was as if he had just driven a stake into my heart.

"She and Jagger now hang out with me all the time," he continued in my face. "They watch me at practice and games. I'm more popular than ever—a king of both the insiders *and* the outsiders."

"I'm telling you, your mother is right this time," I tried to warn.

"Well, was my mother right about Alexander and his family?" he asked, referring to the rampant rumors spread throughout Dullsville that the Sterlings were vampires. "She thought they were weird just because they were different."

"So did you," I argued.

"She said they were vampires," he continued, hitting the ball again. "Had the whole town believing they were. Especially you."

"You were the one who made up and spread those rumors. But in this case, maybe you should believe it."

"That Luna is a vampire?"

I paused.

The restaurant went quiet.

Trevor let the pinball bounce against the bumpers and drop through the flippers.

Just then I felt someone behind me. I turned around.

Jagger, in a ripped white Bauhaus T-shirt and black jeans, and Luna in a black and pink minidress and pink fishnets, stood before me, glaring. She was beautiful. She looked like a gothic pixie fairy girl, with skinny pale arms dangling black rubber bracelets, her long cotton white hair flowing over her shoulders and bright blue eyes sparkling. Both stood in front of me like they were ready to extract me from the diner.

"What are you doing here?" she charged.

Suddenly, like a gothic Superman, Alexander appeared by my side. As Luna leaned in to me, Alexander bravely stepped between us.

"Good-bye, Monster Girl," Trevor said, taking Luna's hand. "C'mon, Jagger."

Jagger gave Alexander a deathly stare, then followed the odd couple toward the tables where the soccer snobs were eating.

I leaned against the pinball machine as Trevor sat at the head of the table with Luna and Jagger on either side. The soccer snobs inched away as if the Romanian siblings had rabies. The players continued to avoid eye contact and kept the conversation to themselves.

"We have to get to the treehouse," Alexander whispered. "While Jagger and Luna are still here."

Alexander and I quickly returned to our table to find our order had just arrived.

"What was that about?" Matt asked.

"We have to go," I said, grabbing my purse.

"But we just got our food!" my best friend argued.

"Becky and I can't drink four shakes," Matt said.

I glanced back at Trevor. The star player was shining in his spotlight, back from a cold to save the team. A girl on one side, his new friend on the other. It disgusted me.

"We really have to go—," I repeated.

"Just because Trevor and those guys are over there?" Becky asked.

"Yes," I said, "but not for the reason you think. I'll have to explain it later. Trust me."

Alexander placed a twenty and a ten on the table. "Please, it's on me."

"Our lucky night—we can order burgers now," Becky joked.

I laughed and gave my best friend a quick hug.

While all eyes were glued to Dixie as she took Jagger and Luna's order, Alexander and I snuck out of the diner, past Jagger's hearse, and into the Mercedes.

"We better hurry," I said as we bolted through Henry's backyard.

Alexander and I didn't know how much time we had to remove the coffins before Jagger and Luna returned.

I scaled up the treehouse ladder and Alexander met me inside. When I pulled back the black curtain, the coffins remained as we'd seen them before.

Alexander stood behind Jagger's casket. Then he pushed the coffin with all his might.

Jagger's bed wouldn't budge.

"What's going on?" I asked.

"It's stuck."

"Is something in it? Maybe a dead body?"

"It would have to be several dead bodies. This thing weighs a ton."

Alexander opened the lid. All that remained inside was a rumpled black blanket and white pillow.

He closed the lid and tried to move it again.

"Maybe it's caught on something."

I bent over the opposite end, and together we pushed and pulled as hard as we could.

But the coffin wouldn't move.

"Let's try Luna's," Alexander said, brushing his dark locks away from his face.

I grabbed one end of the pale pink coffin and Alexander held the other. We couldn't lift Luna's coffin off the ground.

Alexander and I searched the hideout for anything we could use as leverage.

"Check this out," I said, pointing to a few nails lying next to Jagger's duffel bag.

"When I think we've thought of everything, so has Jagger," Alexander said, frustrated.

"I don't have any tools with me," I said.

"I think he counted on that," Alexander remarked, gently touching my shoulder.

Just then we heard the sound of a car driving up the road.

Alexander and I quickly escaped from the treehouse as headlights from Jagger's hearse shined on the driveway.

"I've heard about nailing a coffin lid shut, but never the whole coffin!" I said as we made a fast getaway.

Bat Fight

T he following evening, when I headed out the front door to meet Alexander at the Mansion, I found a red envelope lying on the porch. In black letters it read: RAVEN.

Inside, a red note with black typed letters read:

MEET ME AT OAKLEY PARK, Love, Alexander.

How sweet, I thought. A spontaneous romantic interlude in the park. Alexander Sterling was king of planning the most mysterious, meaningful, marvelous dates—a picnic at the Dullsville cemetery; a goth rock dance at Dullsville's Country Club golf course; picking out my kitty, Nightmare, at an abandoned barn.

I imagined arriving at the park, votives surrounding the Oakley Park fountain, bubbles floating from the steaming water, Alexander and I wading in our bare feet, our lips tenderly touching.

Then I wondered, was this note truly from my vampire mate? Unfortunately, since I'd encountered Jagger at the Coffin Club, I had grown suspicious. After all, Jagger had met me in an alley in Hipsterville, appeared in my backyard, and hid in the Mansion's gazebo. Then again, if it was Jagger, he could just show up at my house.

I hopped on my bike in my lacy black knee-length dress and pedaled my heart out to Oakley Park. I raced over the bumpy grass toward the swings. When I reached the fountain, my dream guy wasn't there. I walked my bike over to the picnic benches.

"Alexander?" I called.

All I saw were the flashing lights of lightning bugs.

Then I heard the music of the Wicked

Wiccas being piped in from the outdoor amphitheater.

I walked my bike over to the domed stage where my parents dragged Billy Boy and me to see Dullsville's symphony orchestra play on Sunday nights during the summer. I had preferred sitting alone on the wet grass, listening to the screeching violins in a rainstorm while my parents sought shelter underneath a tree, to watching them canoodle and dance to "The Stars and Stripes Forever."

I coasted down the aisle of the theater. A lit candelabra and a picnic basket were sitting on a black lace blanket, spread out center stage.

I leaned my bike against a cement bench. I raced around the orchestra pit and climbed onstage.

"Alexander?"

I heard nothing.

I searched the wings. I found only chairs and music stands.

I went to center stage and sat on the blanket. I opened the picnic basket. Maybe there was another note telling me to go to a different romantic location. But the basket was empty.

Something felt strange. The crickets turned silent. I stood up and looked around. Still no Alexander.

Then, right in front of me, stood Luna, in a tight black dress with mesh sleeves and pink fingerless gloves, a pastel pink amulet hanging from her neck.

I gasped and stepped back.

"What are you doing here?" I asked her. "I'm supposed to meet Alexander."

"He got a note, too," she said with a wicked grin. "'Meet me at the cemetery. Raven.'"

I glanced around, peering into the wings of the stage, squinting out at the empty seats. Jagger could have been anywhere.

"I'm here alone," she assured me as if she were reading my thoughts.

"I've got to go—," I said.

Luna stepped in front of me, her chunky black boot almost hitting my own. "I think Alexander can wait. After all, he's made me wait for him since I was born."

"I didn't have anything to do with that," I said, referring to the covenant ceremony in Romania where Alexander was supposed to turn her into a vampire. "And Alexander didn't either. He never made that promise."

"Don't defend him," she argued. "Besides, that's not why I'm here."

"Then why are you?"

"I want you to stop seeing Trevor," she said.

"I don't know what you're talking about."

"Don't play dumb with me. I know you visit him at night. And I overheard you at the diner. You told him to beware of me, like I'm some freak!"

"He has the right to know who you really are."

"I was a freak *before* I turned. Now I am normal."

"But you don't even know the real Trevor. Believe me, *he's* the freak."

"I don't remember asking you for your opinion."

"Jagger is not looking out for you. He's not concerned with finding you a soul mate. He's still looking to get back at Alexander."

"Don't talk about my brother like that. You don't know anything about him—or me. You don't even know me."

"I do know Trevor."

Luna's eyes widened. She stuck her hands in their pink fingerless gloves on her almost nonexistent hips.

"Trevor's right. You are jealous!" she accused. "He thinks you are in love with him. And I do, too."

"Then you are as loony as he is! You deserve each other."

"You won Alexander. I have a right to find my own fun."

"This isn't a contest. These are people, not prizes."

Her blue eyes turned red. She stepped so close to me, I could smell her Cotton Candy lip gloss.

"I want you to back off!" she said in my face.

"I want *you* to back off!" I said in her face.

If she was going to push, I was going to push back harder.

"I'm not afraid of you," Luna said.

"I'm not afraid of *anyone*," I replied.

I thought at any minute we were going to have a cat fight—or in our case, a bat fight.

"If you tell Trevor about me," she threatened,

"then I'm going to tell him about you!"

"What about me?"

"That you are a vampire. That we are vampires."

She stepped back and folded her arms, as if triumphant. I didn't know what to say.

"Then tell him," I said finally. "He'll never believe you."

Luna stepped back and gazed at the moon.

"You are probably right," she relented. "I thought I saw you reflected in the Hall of Mirrors. Jagger convinced me it was part of the illusion. I guess I didn't want to accept that Alexander had turned you. It's odd really, not being like everyone else, isn't it?"

I'd never met a girl, or anyone besides Alexander, who acknowledged feeling the same way I did, vampire or not.

"Yes," I agreed.

Luna's dark mood changed. Her stiff shoulders relaxed. Her angry blue eyes softened, looking almost lost, and lonely.

"It's funny," she continued, "how much we have in common. We're not all that different, you and me. I've always been surrounded by real

vampires. Ones that were born to the Underworld. I'm the only one I know who was turned.
Until I met you."

I could see in Luna's soulful eyes that she was
hungering for a connection. She reminded me of
someone who was alone, living on the outside of
life instead of thriving on the inside. She
reminded me of myself.

"It's not fun being an outcast," I said.

Luna smiled a pale pink smile, like a warm
hug was melting her darkened spirit.

She grabbed my hand as she sat down by the
basket. "Sit for a moment."

"I really should go—," I said, resisting her.

"Just for a minute," she pleaded.

I reluctantly sat down on the blanket.

"Tell me, how did you feel when you
turned?" She scooted closer and eagerly leaned in
to me, like we were gossiping at a slumber party.

"How did I feel?" I asked, confused.

"When Alexander bit you."

I paused. If I answered wrong, I could blow
my whole vampire cover. I was alone, onstage with
a vampiress, without my garlic, a stake, or sunlight
to hide behind, and Alexander was waiting for me

miles away at the Dullsville cemetery.

"Please . . . tell me, how did it make you feel?" she repeated.

"Like magic," I whispered.

"Yes," she nodded eagerly.

"Like a life force I'd never known coursed through my veins and pulsed straight to my heart."

"Go on."

"I felt my heart stop, as if it had exploded with love, then beat again like it never had before," I said, getting caught up in my own imagination, almost believing it myself.

"Me too. . . . But you were in love."

"Yes. I've loved Alexander since the first moment I saw him," I said truthfully.

"He is gorgeous." Then she whispered, as if she were sharing a secret, "I had a fling."

"Who was he?"

"An acquaintance of Jagger's. I barely knew him. But he had a chiseled chin and a ripped chest. Deep blue eyes and spiky red hair like fire. He took me to a warehouse. We made out for a while, his lips were like velvet. And before I knew it, he had bitten me."

"Wow," I said, hanging on her every word.

"We were on unsacred ground, so we were not bonded for eternity. I never saw him again."

"That's so sad," I lamented, honestly feeling sorry for her.

"You were lucky; you found Alexander. So you see how important Trevor is to me. When Jagger introduced us and I stared into his heavenly green eyes, I immediately felt a connection. Not only is he handsome and athletic, but as I got to know him, I sensed that he had everything he could ever want but true love. This is what drew me to him. I'm looking for someone to quench my thirst—for all eternity." She fingered the pink amulet. "Jagger has different needs than I do. He hungers for the hunt, lusts for new prey. Finds ecstasy in the transformation of an innocent mortal into a bloodthirsty vampire. But for me, these bottles are growing quite tiresome. The hunt isn't sustaining me. It's flowing blood that I really crave. The sweet taste of red succulent liquid mixing with the salt of my beloved as it drips and dances on his flesh. To know that someone will ache for me as much as I hunger for him and eternally satiate each other. I want someone to satisfy my hunger forever."

"But Trevor's not good enough. You deserve better," I said earnestly.

She looked at me skeptically.

"You need someone who is intelligent. Sensitive. Mature. Courageous."

"He is those things. You don't know him the way I know him."

I knew I should go, that Alexander must be waiting at the cemetery wondering why I hadn't shown. At the same time, there was so much I wanted to know about Luna, about being turned, about becoming a modern-day vampiress. There was so much I wanted to know for myself. And I didn't know when I'd get another chance.

"Do you like being a vampire?" I asked, now the one riveted.

"I've waited for it all my life. Everyone in my immediate family is a vampire. When my younger brother, Valentine, was born, I dreamed that he would be mortal, like me. But when he wasn't, I cursed the day he was born. The last mortal in my family tree was my great-great grandmother, and I never even knew her. I spent my whole life living in the daylight while the rest of my family slept. I was never part of their world."

"How did you cope all alone?" I wondered.

"I tried to mask it by being a bubbly straight-A student, becoming popular with the kids at school. It put a strain on Jagger's and my relationship. I was jealous of Jagger and he was of me."

"Really? I can't imagine Jagger being jealous of anyone."

"I could see it in his face every time he awoke from his coffin. We had only a few hours together before I had to get to sleep. We'd sit in my bright pink room and I'd share every detail of my events that day at school."

"Who would want to go to school?" I asked.

"Jagger was especially interested in sports. In Europe, soccer is huge. He dreamed of being what he couldn't be—a soccer star. He would show up at night games, hungry to be a player instead of a spectator. But to the students he was odd—a kid who never went to school, was pale and skinny, and dressed like a freak. He was never included. Now he watches Trevor play soccer, wishing he had that life. I think that's why he wants Trevor for me."

For a moment Jagger and Luna weren't vampires but just teens like me who were tired of being outsiders.

"How do you like being a vampire?" she asked.

"Uh . . . I love it," I fibbed.

"But now you're different from your entire family."

"If you'd ever seen my family, you'd know I always was," I said with a laugh.

Luna laughed, too. It was like we'd known each other for years instead of only a few minutes.

"My little brother is a total nerdo," I said, desperate to share my life with her.

"How old is he?"

"Eleven."

"So is Valentine! It's so refreshing to meet someone like you. You understand what it means to live in both worlds but beg for the darker one."

Luna pulled out a Pinky Paranoid clutch purse from behind the basket. "Want some candy?" she asked, handing me a Dynamite Mint.

I nodded and unwrapped the candy as she took out a hair brush. "Tell me about Alexander," she said, inching next to me. She began to brush my hair, as if we'd been soul sisters for years. I felt uncomfortable, as this girly behavior seemed straight out of a Gidget movie. Teens around Dullsville were never seen brushing one another's hair. Luna, however, was much more fairylike than any girl I'd ever met. I felt almost hypnotized and relaxed as she smoothed out my hair, opposite of the way I felt when I was a child and my mom ran a fine-toothed comb through my tangles.

"Alexander's so dreamy. His eyes are like milk chocolates. His attic room is filled with portraits he's painted of me and his family," I rattled on like a drippy girl, then changed my tone. "But it's hard sometimes," I confessed. "I want to share our reflections. I want to have a photo of us on my night stand."

"Yes, it does have its drawbacks. But it's a small price to pay for an eternity together."

Luna pulled my hair off my shoulder and began to braid it.

"Where is the wound from Alexander's bite?" she asked curiously.

I quickly covered my neck with my hand.

She released my hair and raised her white, luxurious locks, exposing two round purple marks on her skinny pale neck.

"They say it takes a year to go away," she said. "I hope it stays there forever."

"Uh . . . it's not on my neck," I teased.

"You are wicked!" she said with a smile, but then turned serious. "I could have sworn Jagger said he saw Alexander bite you on your neck."

"I really have to go," I said, getting up. "Alexander will be worried."

I climbed offstage.

"Wanna hang out again tomorrow?" she asked, following me. "We can meet at sunset."

"I have plans with Alexander," I said, walking up the aisle.

"Then the next night?"

"I'll see," I said, grabbing my bike.

"Why do you need to ride here when you could fly?"

"I have to keep up appearances."

"Good thinking," she said with a wink. "I'll see you later."

I hopped on my bike. "Later!"

I pedaled off. When I turned back to wave, the amphitheater was empty.

I had to admit—I loved being a vampire. Luna not only believed I was part of the Underworld but wanted me as a friend. I felt like I was flying as I raced my bike through downtown and toward my house. I wondered where I would live. Perhaps my understanding parents could remodel our finished basement—board up the windows, remove the white carpeting, and dirty the cement floors with a few bugs and cobwebs. I could sleep in a black coffin with purple seams and silver studs. Or better yet, Alexander and I could live together in the factory with a super-deluxe two-person gothedelic coffin. Plenty of pillows and comfy blankets, with a built-in flat-screen TV in the lid and stereo speakers on the sides.

I pulled into my driveway and found Alexander waiting for me on the front steps, looking as dreamy as ever in black vinyl pants and a ripped black long-sleeve shirt.

"Where were you?" he asked, concerned. "I got your note about meeting you at the cemetery, but you never showed."

"I got a note, too," I said, showing him the red envelope. "To meet you at the park."

"But I didn't write a note."

"I know. Neither did I."

"Then who did?" he asked.

"Your spurned lover."

"Luna? She was never my lover."

"I know. I was just teasing."

"How did you know it was her?"

"She told me. When I showed up at the park."

"Did she hurt you?" he asked.

"She wanted to. It was all a plan to confront me about Trevor. She wants me to stay away from him."

"This is getting out of hand," he said. "I'll talk to her."

"No, she thinks I'm a vampire," I said proudly, placing my hand on his. "Can you believe it? We chatted forever. Like we were best friends."

"Jagger and Luna don't have best friends. We really have to be careful. There's no predicting what they'll do."

"But she really liked me," I insisted.

"I'm sure she did," he said with a smile. "We still can't trust them."

"Well, she trusts me."

"Because you are trustworthy. I know their family, Raven. They're not like you. They are vampires, remember. Real ones."

"She accepts me as a vampire. And Jagger is convinced I am one, too." I paused and looked up at my vampire boyfriend. "And I like it. Why can't *you* accept me as one?"

Alexander's smile turned into a frown. "I accept you as you are. I always have."

He turned away from me.

"I didn't mean to upset you," I said, reaching out to him. I gave him a squeeze with all my might.

"I'm getting so caught up in this, I can't even think straight. You must think I'm so immature."

Alexander softened and caressed my hair.

"You know how I think of you," he said, his chocolate eyes staring into my own. He lifted my chin and kissed me tenderly.

"I don't know how much longer I can go on like this. When will we be together—just us? And not have to worry about Jagger, Luna, and Trevor?"

"How about now?" he said, suddenly bright. "I wanted you to have this." He handed me a wooden heart-shaped box that had been sitting on the window ledge.

My eyes lit up. "You are so sweet! And here I am being selfish."

I opened the box. Hanging from a silver chain was a pendant—black lips with a small vampire fang.

"It's a vampire's kiss," he said proudly.

"Alexander, it's beautiful. I'll wear it forever."

Alexander unclasped my onyx necklace and replaced it with the priceless one he had made just for me.

He gave me a long, lingering good-night kiss.

"Tell me. Would it be easier if I were a vampire?"

Just then my dad pulled into the driveway.

Alexander quickly stepped back into the shadows.

I waited for my dad to come up the front stairs. "Where did Alexander go? He was just here. I wanted to say hi."

"He had to get home before he turns into a pumpkin."

Exhausted, I walked into my darkened bedroom and switched on my *Edward Scissorhands* lamp.

I almost jumped out of my skin. Sitting on my bed, appearing more sinister than ever, was Jagger.

I let out a scream.

That only made the creepy teen smile.

"Raven? What's wrong?" my mom yelled up from downstairs.

"Nothing," I yelled down to her. "Just stubbed my toe." Then I whispered to Jagger, "What are you doing here?"

"Bats can sneak in anywhere. You should know that by now."

"I want you out of here!" I demanded.

"I won't be long. Luna had a lovely chat with you. She's very excited. She thinks she's found a new best friend."

"Well, maybe she has."

"She said you girls talked about all sorts of girly things. Boys. Hair. Vampire bites."

I caught myself in my dresser mirror's reflection and stepped back.

Jagger played with the nightstand light switch. On. Off. On. Off.

"Stop that!" I warned. Something was missing. "Where's Nightmare?"

I heard scratching coming from my computer desk file drawer.

I raced over and opened it up. "Nightmare!" I said, picking up my black kitten. "You poor girl."

"Odd," he said, leering at me. "She doesn't hiss at you."

"She doesn't hiss at Alexander either," I said, gently stroking her fur. "She has taste."

Jagger lay back on my bed, placing his red Doc Martens on my bedspread. "This is a cozy bed."

"Get your feet off of there!" I scolded,

pushing his shoes off.

Jagger leaned across the bed and pulled up the comforter from the floor.

"Where is your coffin?" he asked. "Not under here."

He rose and slithered over to my closet. He slowly opened my closet door. "Not in here," he remarked. "Maybe you're hiding it under *your dress*," he said with a wicked grin.

"It's in the basement."

"Funny. I didn't see it down there."

My blood boiled. I felt enraged. Jagger had been slinking around my house with my family inside.

"It's hidden. Now get out—"

"Sure, but can you show me something?"

"The door? Or the window?" I opened the curtain and lifted the window.

Jagger remained still.

"Some of Trevor's friends said you showed up at school. Curious, really. A vampire risking the sunlight."

"You'd believe a bunch of soccer snobs? They spread more rumors than the *National Enquirer*."

"Well, then," he said, sizing me up with his mismatched eyes, "I have noticed their penchant for gossip."

I felt a sense of relief, but only for a moment.

"At the drive-in I distinctly remember Alexander bit you on the neck. Blood dripping down your neck like a wild river, the sweet smell permeating the air. But Luna said she didn't see a wound. Maybe I could take a peek."

"You can leave. Now."

He stepped closer, his ice blue and green eyes piercing my soul.

"Show me your fangs and I'll show you mine."

"I only show Alexander," I said, inching back.

"What a waste, really." He took another step, pinning me against my computer desk. "So how do you like living this lie?"

"Lie?"

"Yes, it is a lie," he said, staring straight into my eyes. As if he were going to read my soul. "Pretending to be something you're not."

I gasped and looked away. My heart stopped. I bit my black lip.

I reached behind me, stretching my fingers

across my computer desk in hopes of grabbing something to use as a weapon. At any moment Jagger was going to look into my eyes and hypnotize me and drag me back to Dullsville's cemetery. I fingered Billy Boy's two-ton encyclopedia.

"I think you enjoy being deceitful," he said, gently touching the vampire's kiss necklace. "Making believe to your family that you are still mortal."

I breathed again and released the book.

There was a knock at the door.

"I need my encyclopedia."

"Billy—go away."

"You borrowed it two months ago!"

"Billy. Billy—go away," I said sternly.

Jagger stepped back and I raced around him.

Billy Boy opened the door.

I turned around. The curtains were gently blowing. Jagger was gone.

"Is something wrong? You never call me Billy."

I closed the window, rushed over to my brother, and gave him a quick hug. "I never thought I needed to."

Gothic Fairy

The next evening, as I turned the corner to walk up Benson Hill, I saw a shadowy figure standing by the gate. Never one to retreat, I crept up the broken sidewalk slowly. I didn't want to be startled by Trevor or Jagger.

As I got closer, I saw a gothic fairy girl with long white-and-pink-streaked hair leaning against a tree.

"Luna—what are you doing?"

"Raven," she said, bouncing over and giving me a huge squeeze. "I thought I'd find you here."

"But I'm meeting Alexander," I said, almost apologetically.

"I know, but I thought we could chat for a few."

"I don't want to keep him . . ."

I looked up toward the Mansion. The attic window was dark.

"Well . . . maybe just a sec."

We sat on a few rocks outside the Mansion's gate.

"Trevor has a history test. I won't see him until this weekend. Jagger told me he saw you last night," she confessed.

"Did he tell you where he saw me?" I charged.

"In your bedroom."

"He can't do that again. He could scare my family."

"You did that to Trevor. You snuck into his room."

Luna had a good point. "That was different. I have a reputation."

"Jagger is a tricky one," she said with a hint of pride. "He's been teaching me so many things since I've been turned."

165

"Well, I hope they are good tricks," I warned.

"I love your purse," she said, touching the handle of my *Corpse Bride* clutch. "Can I see?"

"Sure." No one, not even Becky, ever got excited about my clothes or fashion accessories. I was proud to share it with her.

She placed it on her arm and modeled it. "So gloom! I love it."

"Thanks. I ordered it online. Maybe I can get you one."

"I'd kill for one," she said eagerly. "Got any candy? I gave my last piece to you yesterday."

"I should have some gum."

Luna unzipped the purse.

"Be careful, it's a mess in there," I warned.

"Wouldn't be cool any other way," she said with a smile.

I leaned back and watched the stars twinkling overhead.

Luna pulled out a pack of Gabe's Grape Gross-Out Gum.

She removed two sticks and returned the pack to my purse.

I didn't mind her rooting around. I didn't have anything to hide in there. Or did I?

"What's this?" she asked, pulling out Ruby's compact.

My heart stopped.

"What do you need a compact for?" Luna asked skeptically, holding the white plastic compact and stroking the red ruby *R*.

"It's an heirloom," I said, trying to reach for it.

"An heirloom?" she wondered aloud. "It doesn't look that old."

Just then a Mustang drove up the road and stopped in front of the Mansion.

I grabbed the compact and purse and ran to the car.

"Matt! Becky! How are you guys doing?"

"Hey, Raven, what's up?" Matt asked.

"Hi, Beck," I said, smiling.

Luna inched up next to me. "Hi, Beck," she said, also grinning.

Becky's smile was strained. My normally amiable best friend looked at me with disdain.

"I thought you were hanging out with Alexander," Becky said.

"I am; I'm just on my way in."

"We just had to have a girl chat before," Luna chimed in.

I was annoyed. There was no need for Luna to try to make Becky jealous.

"I better go see Alexander now," I finally said. "I'll see you tomorrow, Becky."

"Yeah," she said.

I stepped away from the car. Luna put her arm around me and waved at Becky.

Becky politely waved back.

The Mustang headed down the windy road. Alexander had warned me about the motives of Jagger and Luna.

"Bye, Luna," I said, heading for the Mansion as she waited by the street.

This time I was the one to disappear.

The next day the usually early-bird Becky was late. I had showered, eaten, dressed, redressed, and was sitting on the front steps, my hoodie tied around my waist, writing Alexander love notes. I was ready to call the school day off when she finally drove up my driveway.

I got into her pickup, and she barely said hello.

"Where were you?" I asked. "Did you over-sleep? Or get halfway to school and realize you didn't pick me up?"

Becky didn't answer but continued to drive toward school.

After a polite conversation with her responses being "uh-huhs," "sures," and head nods, I'd had enough.

"So what's up with the silent treatment?" I finally asked.

"Nothing," she said as she turned the truck onto the road that led to school.

"Aren't you feeling well?"

"I'm feeling fine."

"Then why are you mad?"

"I'm not mad," she said, and turned up the radio.

I turned the radio off. "Okay. Let me have it. What's up?"

Becky pulled into an empty spot next to the senior parking lot and turned off the engine.

"It just seems odd," she began softly. "You left Hatsy's as soon as our order arrived. Then shortly afterward Jagger and Luna left too. I heard you hung out with Luna at the park. And it was like you were best buds last night outside the Mansion."

"She's not my best bud."

"I know you have way much more in common with her," she continued. "The gothic clothes. The dark music. She probably loves vampires, too."

"Is that what this is about?"

If there was anything worse than the jealousy between sweethearts, it was the threat of a new best friend.

"You've found someone more like you," she said as she got out of the truck.

"I don't want someone more like me," I said as we walked toward school. "I want someone just like you."

In all the years Becky and I'd been friends, she never judged the clothes I wore or the music I listened to. Becky never asked me to be anything but myself.

"You want to know the truth?" I asked.

"Of course."

"You are right, I owe you that." Becky and I went into the side entrance and snuck underneath the staircase. "All right, here goes."

Becky looked anxious, as if I were going to hit her with "Yes, I've found a new best friend. Good riddance."

"This is top secret stuff," I began.

"Go on."

"All right." I took a deep breath. "Here goes. Luna and Jagger are vampires," I began in a whisper, "and they are trying to turn Trevor into one. We left Hatsy's because Alexander and I were trying to remove their coffins from Henry's treehouse, forcing them back to Romania." I sighed, feeling a sense of relief at finally being able to share my darkest secrets with my best friend.

Becky studied me. Then she burst out laughing. "You expect me to believe that?"

"Well—"

"I guess it was better than saying Luna and Jagger are friends of Alexander's from Romania," she said, "and you felt obligated to help out."

"Yeah," I lied. "Sweet, but anticlimactic."

The two of us laughed.

"I'm sorry. I just got a little jealous," she said.

"I'm sorry I made you feel that way. We'll always be best friends."

"Forever," she confirmed.

"For eternity," I added with a smile.

I was shoving my notebooks in my locker, which was filled with pictures of Marilyn Manson, Slipknot, and HIM, and stickers of black roses, spiders, and coffins, when I noticed Trevor passing out red flyers to the soccer snobs and cheerleaders. He was also taking pictures of them with his camera phone.

I wasn't aware Trevor had returned to school. I stepped back into a doorway so Trevor wouldn't spot me.

The bell rang and the crowds began to disperse.

A red flyer fell out of the goalie's notebook as he stepped into a biology classroom. Curious, I grabbed it. In black letters the flyer read:

Graveyard Gala
Covenant Ceremony
~Dare to dance among the dead~

Date: This Saturday
Time: Sunset
Attire: Nightmarish costume

Be there or be dead

I'd spent a whole lifetime partying alone at Dullsville's cemetery. Now all of Dullsville High was going to be at my hideout. And I wasn't even invited?

"Sticking your nose where it doesn't belong, Monster Girl?" I heard Trevor say from behind me.

"What's this?" I asked, shoving the flyer in his face.

"Jagger's hosting a party. It'll be the blowout of the year! I'm coming as the Grim Reaper. You're lucky. If you were invited, you could just come as yourself."

I gave Trevor a snarled look.

"Who is going to have a covenant ceremony?"

"Luna and I will be king and queen of the covenant. Like a medieval prom, in ominous costumes. It's a sexy Romanian ceremony I'm sure you've never heard of. When I accept the honor, Luna's going to kiss me in front of the whole school. It's going to be a total freakfest. But since you're not on the guest list," he continued, "you'll have to read about it in the school newspaper."

He grabbed the flyer out of my hand as a cheerleader and a soccer snob stepped in front of me.

Just then Trevor aimed his cell phone at them and a flash illuminated the hallway, momentarily blinding me.

When my eyes finally adjusted, Trevor and his cohorts disappeared into the crowd of students.

I stood in the hallway, motionless, surrounded by the sounds of closing lockers and classroom doors.

This had been Jagger's plan all along! The only way he could lure someone as conservative as Trevor to the sacred ground of a cemetery was the promise of a monster-size party and a never-ending lip-lock. The already pompous soccer snob would be sealing the deal with the gorgeous "new hottie" in front of the whole school. Trevor just didn't realize the deal would last an eternity.

"Raven," I heard Becky call from behind.

Becky and Matt pushed through the crowd of students and caught up to me.

"Did you hear about the Graveyard Gala?" she asked. "Seems like you would be the one handing out invites, not Trevor."

"I know. And to top it off, I'm not even invited. Not like I've ever been on the A-list before, but this is at a cemetery. My dream party!"

"I thought you would freak out!"

"Since you told Trevor to hit the road, the three of us are probably the only ones not invited."

Then I spotted a red flyer poking out of Matt's algebra textbook.

"You were on the guest list?" I asked, horrified.

"The whole soccer team is invited," Matt said.

"But you're not going, are you?" I asked.

"I have to," Matt confessed. "I don't want to be the only one in the locker room who wimped out."

"And you?" I said, turning to my best friend.

"Matt needs a date," she said apologetically.

I felt betrayed. Everyone at Dullsville High was going but me. Even Becky. More important, though, I was worried about Becky—I didn't want my best friend on sacred ground with vampires.

"Well, Becky, you can't go," I said, sounding like her parent. "Cemeteries make you nervous."

"I'll be there to protect her from any wayward ghosts," Matt said, putting his arm around my smiling friend.

Then I remembered the cemetery's caretaker and his dog. "Old Jim will be there with his Great Dane, Luke," I warned Becky.

"There won't be trouble," Matt said. "Trevor has assured everyone that on Saturday nights Old Jim has a barstool with his name on it at Lefty's Tavern."

"Promise me you'll come," Becky pleaded. "I'd feel better if you were there, too."

"You thought I wouldn't be there? And miss the chance to crash a party?" I said, opening a classroom door. "Only in my nightmares!"

I waited impatiently at the Mansion's front door as the sun fell into the horizon. Hues of lilac, lavender, fuchsia, and pink brushed across the sky. I wished I could share it with Alexander.

Soon I heard the Mansion locks opening and saw the iron doorknob turn. Alexander, handsomely dressed in a black-and-gray pinstripe silk shirt, black dress pants, and silver-flamed Gibsons greeted me.

"You look gorgeous," I complimented, stepping inside. "I've got major news!"

"So do I," Alexander said quickly. He gave

me a sweet kiss on the cheek and closed the door behind me.

A delicious smell of grilled steak permeated the entranceway.

"Me first," I began, excited.

Jameson hurried out from the kitchen carrying a serving tray of seasoned red potatoes. He placed it on the dining-room table, which was set for four.

"Hello, Miss Raven," Jameson said brightly, greeting me. "Allow me to take your jacket."

Confused, I reluctantly unzipped my black Emily the Strange sweatshirt hoodie.

"Everything is ready," Creepy Man said, taking my hoodie and hanging it in the hallway closet. "All we need is the guest of honor."

"What's going on?" I asked. "We need to talk—"

"Jameson invited Ruby to join us for dinner."

"Us?"

Alexander nodded.

"What a nice surprise," I said with a cheesy grin.

Normally I would have been ecstatic to be included in a dinner party at the Mansion with

Alexander, the creepy butler, and the fabulous Ruby White. But we didn't have time for pleasantries and pastries when we had to think of a new plan to foil Jagger and Luna.

"I want everything to be perfect," Jameson said, straightening the black lace tablecloth. "I thought it would be easier if Miss Raven were here too. Miss Ruby might feel more comfortable in the Mansion."

"I don't mean to be rude," I whispered to Alexander as Jameson headed back to the kitchen.

"I know, it's a surprise to me, too. I barely had enough time to get you these," he interrupted.

Alexander picked up a pewter vase with three black roses and handed it to me.

I melted. I looked into his caring midnight eyes. For a moment I forgot about any other vampires except for mine.

"We have to talk," I said. "Jagger is—"

Just then there was a knock at the Mansion door.

Jameson burst out of the kitchen holding an elegantly wrapped white orchid and headed for the door. "I'll get it; you two settle in. . . ."

I couldn't settle anything. My heart was racing. My mind was restless. My stomach was doing flip-flops.

Jameson opened the front door. Ruby stepped inside, dressed in white pleated dress pants, a tailored cotton-colored blazer with a white lingerie top, and cream Prada pumps. She was clutching a Coach bag and a bottle of white wine.

Ruby's eyes lit up when she saw Jameson holding the flower. She nervously giggled as the odd couple exchanged the orchid and the aging Chardonnay.

"A white orchid!" she exclaimed. "Jameson, you didn't have to go to all the trouble," she said, her voice melting.

"A rare flower for someone as rare as you . . . ," the skinny butler complimented.

Ruby's eyes lit up and she gave him a kiss on the cheek. Creepy Man's deadly complexion turned bright cherry red.

"Hello, Raven," she said, giving me a quick hug. "I'm glad I get to see you again so soon."

"I know, isn't this wonderful?" I agreed with a Cheshire cat grin.

"Thank you, Alexander, for having me over," Ruby continued. "I've always wanted to see the Mansion from the inside."

"Jameson can give you the grand tour," Alexander hinted so we could get a chance to talk.

"After dessert," Jameson said.

"I left something upstairs, Raven—," Alexander began.

"It will have to wait," Jameson ordered. "Dinner is served."

Alexander and I had no choice but to follow Ruby and Jameson into the dining room. Several candelabrum and silver candlesticks gently lit the darkened room, revealing a long oak table covered with a black lace tablecloth. Antique china, pewter goblets, and ancient silver utensils were set in front of each chair. Crystal glasses were filled with water. A few cobwebs still hung from the corners of the gigantic ceiling. The heavy red velvet drapes seemed to have been hanging there since the Mansion was built.

Ruby must have felt as if she were going to have dinner with the Munsters.

Jameson stood at the head of the table and

offered an antique chair for Ruby while Alexander pulled out the adjacent chair for me.

I could get used to this. I felt like I was at a five-star restaurant. Normally at home, Billy Boy and I were on top of each other, fighting for the chair by the TV.

Alexander sat across from me. With the Frankenstein-size oak table and a huge white flowered centerpiece between us, it would be impossible to whisper my findings to him now.

Jameson uncorked Ruby's bottle and began to fill her goblet. I could see his hands shake as he tried not to spill any wine on her perfectly pressed ultraswank white outfit.

Alexander grabbed a red bottle sitting on a serving cart next to him and poured red liquid into his glass.

Ruby signaled Jameson to stop pouring her wine. "I didn't know you were serving steak. You can save this bottle for another time," she offered. "I'll just have what Alexander's drinking."

Alexander and Jameson paused, gravely glancing at each other.

"Uh . . . I think you'd prefer your

Chardonnay," Alexander suggested.

Jameson grinned a toothy grin. "Alexander's on a strict vitamin regimen. That's his special drink."

"It's like drinking blood," I whispered, rolling my eyes.

Ruby wrinkled her forehead. "Then I'll stick with what I have," Ruby said.

We began to drink our various libations while Jameson kindly placed well-done steaks in front of Ruby and me. Jameson then set a plate before Alexander—an almost rare filet, the meat oozing blood-red juice.

As Alexander, Jameson, and I began to eat our dinners, Ruby intently watched Alexander eat his juicy steak like she was watching a juggler swallow fire.

"That's how they eat steak in Romania," I whispered.

"I've been to Romania," she quietly responded. "I guess I must have visited a different region."

I glanced at Alexander, who was eating quickly. A nervous Jameson barely touched his food. Ruby ate slowly, savoring her dinner.

We made unbearable small talk and complimented our chef on the meal.

The candles flickered. Shadows danced about the room. The wind howled through the trees. With the four of us sitting around the table, I felt at any moment we were going to hold hands and perform a seance. All that was missing was the Ouija board.

The wax slowly dripped from the candlesticks. *Drip. Drip. Drip.* Like the ticking of a grandfather clock. This evening could go on forever.

"This Mansion is very . . . historic," Ruby said, trying to find a polite word. "Have you seen any ghosts?"

"Just my grandmother," Alexander said.

Ruby choked on her wine. "Excuse me?"

"This house used to belong to Alexander's grandmother," Jameson tried to explain. "But we never—"

"So you've really seen her?" I asked eagerly.

"She wanders through the halls at night," Alexander said in a low voice. "In fact . . . she's standing right behind you!"

I laughed, but Ruby jumped up from her seat

as if she'd just seen the ghost herself.

Alexander and Jameson immediately rose from their chairs.

"I didn't mean to frighten you," Alexander apologized.

"Are you all right?" Jameson asked, offering her water. "Alexander gets these ideas. . . ."

Ruby was embarrassed. "I'm just not used to being in a house that's—"

"Haunted?" I asked.

"Large," she corrected. "And dark; I usually have all the lights on," she said with a forced laugh.

"We can light more candles," Alexander offered.

"Please. Sit, sit. And not another word," she said.

Jameson slowly returned to his seat and we continued eating our dinners. "So, Miss Raven, anything unusual happen at school?" he asked, politely trying to redirect the conversation.

"Other than that I showed up?"

My dinner mates laughed as if grateful for some comic relief.

"Well, a guy at school was talking about

sneaking into the cemetery."

"The cemetery? That sounds like something you'd do," Ruby said with a laugh.

"He's not just sneaking in," I said, and then turned to Alexander. "He's going there on a date."

"Who would take a date to the cemetery?" Ruby asked, horrified.

Then Ruby eyeballed me and the other gloom-and-doom diners dressed in black around her.

We all stared back.

"Not me," I burst out.

"I wouldn't be caught dead," Alexander admitted.

"Poor taste!" Jameson proclaimed.

We quickly returned to our meals.

"Miss Raven, maybe I should have asked if you discussed anything *usual*," Jameson said nervously.

I politely laughed. But I had more info I had to share.

"Did I mention he's planning to kiss his girl-friend next to a coffin?" I said to Alexander.

Ruby cleared her throat.

"More water?" Jameson asked, clearly worried we were upsetting his guest of honor.

"I'm fine," she answered.

Alexander stared off behind Ruby and started pointing.

"Now are you going to tell me you see a ghost behind me?" she asked.

Alexander shook his head. "It's worse."

"I'm not falling for your tricks again," she said with a grin.

"Don't move," Alexander said, putting his napkin on the table.

Ruby slowly turned around. Hanging from the red velvet curtain right above her was a bat.

She wasn't even fazed. "I bet it's made out of rubber," she said, and got up.

Jameson called out, "Miss Ruby!"

My eyes bulged. Alexander rose.

"I'll show you," she said confidently.

Just then Ruby reached for the bat. All at once, it spread its wings wide and took off.

Ruby let out a bloodcurdling scream so loud I had to cover my ears.

The disgruntled bat flew around the room as Ruby hid behind me, continuing to shriek.

"Does it have blue and green eyes?" I asked, shielding her.

"Who cares about its eye color!" she yelled.

Alexander tried to grab the bat, but it only flew higher.

"I'm going to faint!" she hollered. "I'm really going to faint."

Jameson and I helped a trembling Ruby away from the dining room and into the sitting room.

"Is it in my hair?" she asked, now sitting in a green Victorian chair.

"No," I reassured her.

"Where did it go?"

"It's in the other room. Alexander is going to catch him."

"Are there more?" she asked, her shaking hands covering her head.

"No, they live in the attic tower, far away from this room." Jameson tried to comfort his date with a glass of water. "I wonder how he got down here."

"I almost touched it!" she exclaimed. "I almost touched a rat with wings!"

Alexander came into the room holding a balled up linen napkin.

"He's completely harmless, see?" Alexander asked, innocently opening the napkin. Two beady black eyes stared back at us.

Ruby let out another bloodcurdling scream.

"Please take it away!" a haggard Jameson pleaded.

"Aww, he's cute," I said as Alexander walked out to the kitchen to set it free.

"I guess this means you're not staying for dessert," Jameson said.

"I'm stuffed, really," Ruby said, still in shock. "Besides, I have to open the office tomorrow." She rose from her seat.

"I understand," Jameson responded, his head hung low. He retrieved Ruby's purse and the flower from the hallway table and handed them to her.

"Thank you," she said quickly. "The orchid is beautiful. The dinner was delicious." Still shaken, Ruby headed for the door.

"The evening didn't go as I had planned," Jameson confessed sorrowfully, following her. "You are used to the finer things, Miss Ruby. I was wrong to think—"

"That's okay," she said softly. "I understand."

I knew Jameson had invited Alexander and me to dinner to make Ruby more comfortable. Instead we spent the whole evening talking about cemeteries and coffins. I felt awful.

"Please don't blame Jameson," I begged. "It's my fault Alexander and I talked about creepy things and spooked you. Jameson is a perfect gentleman."

"It's nobody's fault," she reassured. "I guess we were all a bit nervous."

"Then how about dinner tomorrow night?" I suggested.

"Well . . . ," Ruby began hesitantly.

"At a bright, trendy restaurant with upbeat music?" I continued.

"That might be nice," she relented.

"Just the two of you," I said.

"Just the two of us," Jameson eagerly agreed.

"And no mention of coffins, ghosts, or flying bats," I added.

"Well . . . it's a date," Ruby concurred with a smile.

Jameson opened the door for Ruby. He turned back to me and smiled a skinny-toothed smile and winked.

"From now on," I overheard him say to Ruby as he walked her to her car, "the only bats you'll see is when I invite you to a baseball game."

The Grim Plan

Alexander and I grabbed the savory desserts Jameson had made—placinta, fried sweet dough filled with chocolate—and headed up to the privacy of his attic room. "Trevor is taking Luna to the cemetery?" Alexander immediately asked, shutting the door.

"Jagger is planning a Graveyard Gala on Saturday night," I blurted out as we sat with our placintas on his mattress. "It's a gothic costume party with the highlight of the evening being a covenant ceremony. Instead of luring Trevor to sacred ground alone," I started, too excited to dive into my treat, "Jagger is inviting Dullsville High. Luna is going to bite Trevor in front of everyone—only no one will know what's going to happen, not even Trevor himself."

"How will he not know what's going on?"

"Trevor thinks he's going to be kissed by Luna, not bitten."

"They are going to be wearing costumes, right?" Alexander asked.

"Yes, Trevor is going as the Grim Reaper. It will be dark and all the partygoers will be wearing masks. While they drink, dance, and make out, Luna will finally have her long-awaited covenant ceremony. No one will know what is really happening."

"Then we have to stop Trevor from going," Alexander said, picking at his dessert.

"He wouldn't miss this for the world. He will be the star of the show."

"Then we have to tell him what the ceremony really is."

"He'll never believe me. Besides, they've already passed out flyers. With all of Dullsville High on sacred ground, Luna could easily take someone else."

"Then she'll have to believe she is with Trevor."

"Believe? Who will she really be with?"

"Me. I'll be dressed as the Grim Reaper, too. I'll be covered from head to toe. Luna won't know the difference."

"But you told me if a vampire takes another on sacred ground, then they are theirs for eternity. I don't want her to bite you and then I lose you forever."

"I don't either," he said, and squeezed my hand. "But when I take off my hood, she'll know Trevor has gone."

"Where will he be?"

"Safe, off sacred ground. At some point you'll have to distract him and lead him out of the cemetery," Alexander explained.

"I'm used to distracting people, just not on purpose. I hope everything goes smoothly. The whole school will be on sacred ground with two vengeful vampires."

"Bring some garlic just in case, and I'll take my antidote."

"I don't want to give you another shot," I said.

"Hopefully, you won't have to."

S hortly after sunset Alexander and I walked up the lonely road that led to Dullsville's cemetery. Although I wasn't actually a vampire, I felt like I was. I'd convinced twin vampires I was as undead as they were, I was on the arm of the most handsome of vampires, and I was going to party with a bunch of other ghouls. I was happy to be me—vampire or not.

I was dolled up as Elvira, in a long black dress with shredded spidery sleeves and a slit racing up my leg, exposing black mesh tights. Long black plastic fingernails flashed from my pale fingertips. My jet black hair was teased up like a fountain, the ends falling down over my shoulders. I revealed as much cleavage as I could manage to squeeze out in a recently purchased push-up bra. I'd also bought Alexander the last Grim Reaper costume left over from Halloween merch at Jack's department store. It was a black hooded costume with a skeleton mask and a plastic scythe.

"You look stellar," Alexander said, his midnight eyes sparkling as we walked together. "I can't believe I'm with you."

It was a dream come true for me to be strolling down the street holding the bony skeleton hand of the Grim Reaper—and even doubly dreamy that it was really my vampire boyfriend.

Cars lined the street leading up to the cemetery. At the far end of the road, parked alongside a Dumpster, I saw Jagger's hearse.

I was as excited as I was nervous to implement our plan.

When we turned the corner to the cemetery, Alexander said, "I brought my antidote. Did you bring your garlic?"

I stopped dead in my tracks. "I knew I forgot

something!" I exclaimed. "It's in my night stand. We have to go home," I pleaded.

"We don't have time," Alexander warned. "The ceremony could be over by the time we'd return."

We reached the iron gate and climbed over the fence. When we were safely on the cemetery ground, I saw a sight I'd never seen before—and one thing we hadn't planned on. The graveyard was filled with Grim Reapers.

"How will we ever find Trevor now?" I asked. "It will take forever!"

My heart sank as I stepped over cans of soda littering the graveyard. I bent down to pick up an empty can.

"We don't have time for that now," Alexander said again. "If we don't get to Trevor in time, the caretaker and the rest of Dullsville will have to worry about more than empty cans and bottles."

We passed a Grim Reaper who was talking to a werewolf. "Trevor?" I asked, but the Angel of Death shook his head.

We passed ghosts and ghouls dancing and drinking among the tombstones.

Sitting on a wooden bench was a familiar witch holding hands with Michael Myers.

"You are quite the spooky pair," I said.

"Raven," the witch said as the two rose. "I'm so glad you came."

"Wow, that is some dress," Matt said from underneath his hockey mask. "Maybe you could get a costume like that for Becky."

My best friend turned devil red.

"This party is great," Matt continued. "The whole school is here."

"We're looking for Trevor. Have you seen him?" I asked.

"No. Word has it that he's going to be in some medieval ceremony by the tombs in just a few minutes."

Then I noticed Luna a few yards ahead, placing a flower at the base of Alexander's grandmother's monument.

"Do me a favor; if things get weird, will you go home?" I whispered to Becky.

"We are partying in a cemetery," she said. "Things are *already* weird."

I gave Becky a quick hug, and Alexander and I headed for the monument.

Luna stood up. She was beautiful—like a gothic prom fairy. She glowed in a ghostly white tattered prom dress, with a pink wrist carnation and combat boots. Her soft hair flowed over her shoulders like a waterfall; her frost white complexion, highlighted by heavy indigo eye shadow and pale pink lip gloss, glistened softly.

"Trevor said you weren't coming," Luna exclaimed, bouncing over to us like a butterfly. "But I knew you'd come."

"We weren't invited," I said, "but I wouldn't let that stop me. I wouldn't want to miss your covenant ceremony for the world."

"Look at what you missed in Romania," she said proudly to Alexander. She was beautiful as she giggled and did a flirty spin, modeling her tattered dress for him.

Alexander wasn't amused.

"Where's Trevor?" he asked. "Is he getting cold feet?"

"No, but he thinks I have his cold. When we met here tonight, I started to feel ill. Sweet, really. A vampire with a cold," she said with a grin. "So he went to his car to get me cough drops. He's dressed as the Grim Reaper," she remarked in a spooky voice.

"I know," I said. "So is everyone else."

"Stay here with me," Luna begged, taking my hand.

"We'd better find Trevor," I told her. "We need to start the ceremony before the cops get wind of this party."

She relaxed her grip. "You're right," she said. "Please hurry."

"Alexander, would you stay with me?" she asked sweetly.

I grabbed my boyfriend's arm. "Alexander has to come with me. I'll need him to help me find Trevor."

"Man, she really must still like you," I said as we walked past the tombs. "I had to pry her bony fingers off of you."

Alexander and I headed for Trevor, but we didn't know where to begin. The graveyard was full of Angels of Death.

We saw two Grim Reapers playing spin the bottle with a few cheerleaders dressed as red devils.

"Trevor?"

"Over there," one said, pointing her pitchfork

toward the front of the cemetery.

"I'll wait a few minutes and double back as Trevor," Alexander said. "Make sure he gets out of the cemetery grounds. And I want you to stay away, too."

"So you can stand up there on sacred ground alone with two vampires?"

"I can't protect both me *and* you." Alexander lifted his skeleton mask from his face.

His charcoal eyes sparkled. He leaned in and kissed me.

"I'm going to double back now," he said, replacing his mask.

I waited for a moment and watched as the man of my dreams confidently, and selflessly, set forth on our mission.

"Trevor!" I called as I ran through the cemetery.

I caught up with one reaper.

"Trevor?"

"No, but I'm sure he's around," a girl's voice mumbled.

I raced toward the front gate. I looked for any Grim Reaper carrying cough drops.

Then I wondered, maybe Luna was making

up the story. Maybe Trevor had been at the ceremony the whole time.

"Trevor?" I desperately asked a Grim Reaper heading straight for me.

"Yes, Monster Girl?" He crossed his arms, his heavy, billowy sleeves hanging down.

My eyes lit up. Now that I had Trevor, I had to get him off sacred ground.

"I finally found you!"

A stone-cold skeleton mask stared back at me.

"Uh . . . Luna is still not feeling well," I rambled. "Allow me to escort you to get her cough drops."

I took his white skeleton hand and tried to lead him toward the gate.

The Angel of Death didn't follow.

Instead he held up a pack of vitamin C with his bony hand. He turned away from me and headed for the ceremony.

I raced after him.

"I've been trying to tell you," I began. "Luna isn't the girl you think she is. She's not some nice straight-A cheerleader. She's going to double-cross you."

He shook his head and walked on.

"Trevor. You can't!"

When I caught up to him, I grabbed the sleeve of his costume. With a quick jerk, he pulled his arm away.

I was on a mission, impossible as it might be. I grabbed his plastic scythe, but he continued to walk on.

I raced ahead, blocking his way with the scythe.

"Wait," I whispered, out of breath. "Please, before you go any further. You were the one who tried to convince the town about the Sterlings. Why don't you see Alexander in the daylight? Why did Luna and Jagger invite you to a cemetery? You were right all along. They weren't rumors. It was all because they *are* vampires."

I stared at his fixed skeleton face. He waved his skeleton hand and pushed his way past me. I followed him back to the site of the covenant ceremony.

A crowd of aliens had already gathered in front of the tomb. Ghosts and witches were everywhere, standing, sitting, leaning.

In front of the tombs was a coffin with a lit candelabra. Alexander, passing as Trevor in his

Grim Reaper costume, was waiting on one side with a pewter goblet.

With all my might, I grabbed the arm of the Angel of Death standing next to me. "Don't go," I begged. "Please. Alexander is up there, trying to divert their vicious plan. Watch what happens, and if I'm wrong then *I'll* kiss you right here in front of the whole school!" I blurted out.

He stopped and looked at me for a few long seconds.

My heart ceased. I realized what I had just committed to. Our plan had better work. I held all our lives *and* my mouth at stake here.

We hid behind some partygoers, standing a few feet from Alexander.

Then I saw Luna walking up the cemetery aisle, gravestones on either side of her, a dead bouquet in her hand.

Becky and Matt snuck in next to me.

"This is cool. It's like a creepy gothic wedding," the friendly witch said. "Maybe we can be next," she teased Matt.

I yanked the Angel of Death back. "I've tried to tell you all along," I said in a whisper. "You were right about the Sterlings. They are vampires.

And so are Luna and Jagger. Please believe me. Before it's too late."

Alexander drank from the goblet.

Luna reached my Grim Reaper and drank from the goblet too. Then she said something inaudible.

"What did she say?" Becky asked.

"'To the king and queen of the graveyard,'" Matt repeated.

Luna turned to Alexander. She leaned in to him.

I gasped. The crowd cheered.

"No!" I shouted, lunging forward, but a cadaverous hand stopped me.

I turned to see the Angel of Death behind me.

Just then Alexander grabbed Luna's shoulders and held her at arm's length.

"What are you doing? Don't push me away!"

"Kiss her! Kiss her!" the crowd chanted.

But Alexander kept the vampiress at bay with one hand. He pulled off his reaper's hood.

"I'm not Trevor!" Alexander exclaimed. "Now you can stop your games."

"Why is Alexander there?" Matt said to

Becky. "What's going on?"

Luna glared at my true love. She started to laugh. "It was never Trevor I wanted here. It was you!"

Alexander stepped back, confused. Luna grabbed his oversized sleeve. "Now I don't have to wait for you to take me. I can take *you*!"

I lunged forward, but the Angel of Death squeezed my shoulder.

"Get off!" I ordered.

Thank goodness Alexander was stronger than the waifish Luna. He held his scythe in one hand and the writhing vampiress at bay with the other.

On the far side of Luna a Grim Reaper pushed through the crowd toward the struggling vampires.

"Luna, what are you doing?" he yelled. "This wasn't the plan. You are not supposed to be with Alexander!"

The crowd cheered, "Fight! Fight!"

Alexander began to cough, letting go of Luna.

"This is who I've always wanted," Luna defended. "Alexander is who I've waited my life for." She coughed, too, and clung to the side of the coffin.

The hooded reaper yanked off his shroud. Blond hair flung down over his face. It wasn't Jagger. Standing in between Luna and Alexander was Trevor Mitchell.

I stepped back, shocked. If Trevor, Luna, and Alexander were struggling by the coffin, whose hand was on me?

I inched away and tried to release my hand. The Angel of Death only squeezed harder. Then he pulled me a few feet away from the ceremony.

I turned and tore off the reaper's black hood. Blue and green eyes stared back at me. It was Jagger.

"You aren't going anywhere, Monster Girl," he said with a seductive, menacing voice.

My vampire boyfriend grew red with rage as he saw Jagger by my side on sacred ground. "Raven!" Alexander called. He started to wheeze and began to stagger toward us.

Trevor glanced over, shocked and confused.

I tried to pull my hand away, but Jagger tightened his grip and started to cough.

Alexander was doubling over but was determined to reach me. "Jagger, let her go!" he warned.

With every step Alexander took forward, Jagger took one back.

The confused crowd started cheering. Some shouted, "Kiss! Kiss!" while others yelled, "Fight! Fight!"

Luna recoiled from the confused and rejected Trevor, her pasty complexion turning even paler.

Jagger's eyes began to tear. His breathing became labored.

What could be making all the vampires ill?

Then it hit me. The vampires began to get sick when Trevor showed up.

"What's wrong with Alexander?" I heard Becky ask Matt.

"Trevor's taken garlic pills!" I shouted to Alexander. "Take your antidote," I said, pointing to my leg.

Alexander wheezed but reached underneath his cloak and pulled out his serum. Becky and Matt ran to his side while Alexander jammed the shot into his leg.

Jagger backed up, pulling me farther away

from the crowd.

"Get off of me," I said wedging my boot between us.

"Not so fast," he said with hypnotic eyes. "Alexander made a fool of our family in Romania, and you were planning to do it again tonight?"

"Let me go—"

"Where's your vampire bite, Raven?" he whispered.

"I told you, I can't show you."

"You were very convincing. Until Luna discovered a compact mirror in your purse. You led her on; you led us both on."

"I did not!"

"Then why aren't you wheezing now? And most important, what's this?" He reached underneath his cloak and pulled out a cell phone. He flipped the phone open and held it before me— a picture of a cheerleader and a soccer snob at school, taken by Trevor. And standing in back of them was a mortal Raven, reflecting back for all vampires to see.

"You have a cunning and crafty nature. You turned out to be more of a vampire than

Alexander," Jagger said flatly.

Alexander pushed through the crowd toward us. Trevor followed close behind.

"What is Jagger doing with Raven?" Trevor asked.

"Back off!" Jagger shouted. "You will not make a fool of my family anymore."

"What's he talking about?" Trevor said, now standing by Alexander.

"Get back!" Jagger shouted to Trevor, coughing as he spoke. "You think you have it all with your sports and your pretty girls. But you were never like us and could never be good enough for my sister."

"You planned this all along?" Trevor asked Jagger. "Raven was right, trying to warn me about you for days. Why? Just because I was different?"

Trevor had picked on me all my life because I was the outsider. Now he faced the same ridicule.

"Go back to your soccer field," Jagger said. "This game is way out of your league."

I stared at my mortal nemesis, whose face was growing red with rage. For the first time in sixteen years, Trevor Mitchell had finally met a bigger bully than himself.

Trevor looked at Jagger as if he were a soccer ball that needed to be kicked into the opponent's goal.

"Get off," I said to Jagger. "You're hurting me!"

Alexander's eyes turned red. "Jagger. You have one second to let her go! Otherwise, it's all over!"

Jagger's grip was so hard around my wrist I couldn't move.

"It'll feel like a pin prick," he said to me in a seductive voice. He gently stroked my hair away from my shoulders. He leaned toward me and flashed his fangs.

"No!" I cried.

And the world went black.

18

Cryptic Kryptonite

I awoke, lying flat on my back on the grass, the stars twinkling above me.

"Raven?" Becky asked, her hand outstretched. "Are you okay?

My world was dizzy. I grabbed my neck. "Am I a . . . ?" I asked.

Becky helped me up. "I thought you were kidding when you said they were vampires. I think that Jagger guy really believed he was. He tried to bite you."

I felt my neck for wounds.

Suddenly the memory started to come back. I never thought it would happen. My nemesis and the love of my life, enraged for different reasons, both staring straight at me.

I had spent the last few days trying to save Trevor from the clutches of a vampire and now he, alongside Alexander, unknowingly saved me.

The impact of their tackling Jagger had sent me flying to the ground.

Becky and I now raced the few yards to the tombs, where a huge crowd had gathered. Alexander was standing over Jagger, who was coughing and wheezing. Luna was leaning against the covenant coffin.

Trevor had no idea that the garlic tablet was making them vulnerable. He thought it was his bravado.

The soccer snobs encircled Jagger and Luna.

Matt and Becky stayed by my side. "Alexander's deathly allergic to garlic," I said.

"It looks like Jagger and Luna are, too," Becky remarked. "That and being pummeled by Alexander and Trevor."

"I told Trevor the gelcap was an aphrodisiac," I proudly whispered when I reached Alexander.

"Apparently he told his friends, too," he said softly with a smile. "The entire soccer team must have taken them."

Alexander turned to Jagger and Luna. "It's time you return to Romania. For good."

"Yeah, go back to Romania, you freaks!" Trevor said, balling up his fists.

I put my arm around Alexander's waist and held him close.

Then I turned to Trevor.

"I guess you are the school bully again," I complimented.

Just then a dog started barking, distracting everyone. We all turned around.

"What's going on here?" Old Jim, the caretaker, called, holding a flashlight toward us.

Ghosts and goblins started to jump the fence. Werewolves and witches hid behind tombstones. The soccer snobs took off around the shed. Becky and Matt raced up the cemetery aisle.

"What's with all these cans?" Old Jim scolded. "I'm going to call the police!"

Alexander, Trevor, and I turned back to the coffin.

All that remained was the flickering candelabra.

Jagger and Luna were gone.

19

Vampireville

B ack at Alexander's attic room, after weeks of adventures with the twin vampires behind us, Alexander and I finally had a chance to be alone and chill.

I had a lot of time to make up for in the lip-action department. We cuddled and kissed in his comfy chair until I thought my heart would explode out of my chest. He nibbled playfully on my neck, and I wondered if it was hard to resist my mortal self.

"Anytime you are ready," I offered. "The cemetery is only a few miles away."

"I like you just the way you are," he said, and brushed a few strands of hair from my face. "You know that."

"But you may like me better," I teased.

He began tickling me, and I cried out in laughter. I leaned back and accidentally kicked something hard against the wall.

It was the door handle to his hidden attic room.

I was immediately brought back into the reality of the situation.

"Just for a minute?" I pleaded.

Alexander hesitated.

"After all I've been through. All we've been through. It would mean the world to me," I added.

Alexander paused. His midnight eyes could not mask the dark conflict that he was trying to conquer in his soul. After a moment he rose from the chair and offered me his hand.

Exhilaration rushed through me like I was Veruca Salt about to step into Willy Wonka's chocolate factory.

Alexander pulled out a skeleton key from his pocket, pushed away the comfy chair, and unlocked the secret door.

He slowly opened the entranceway into his cryptic world.

There, as I'd seen a few days earlier, a secret in the shape of a casket—a simple black open coffin with dirt haphazardly sprinkled around it. Next to it there was a wooden table with an unlit half-melted candle and a small, softly painted portrait of me.

I walked inside the room. Alexander followed me and lit the candelabra. The room was sparse—void of a decorative soccer headboard like Trevor's or hanging posters of sports teams like Billy Boy's.

I peered into his coffin: black sheets, a black pillow, and a rumpled blanket.

"I love it. You don't even make your coffin. Just like any teen."

I looked into his lonely eyes, which now sparkled.

Then I noticed something silver lying on the pillow, catching the candlelight. I leaned over and picked it up. It was my black onyx necklace that Alexander had replaced with the vampire's kiss one he'd made for me.

My heart melted as I held it in my hand.

"I sleep better knowing I have a part of you close to me."

No one had ever meant so much to me as Alexander. For my whole life, I'd suffered as an outsider. The fact that because of me he, too, felt less alone in his world was almost too much for this dreamy goth girl to bear.

Tears welled up in my eyes.

"May I?" I asked, motioning to the coffin.

Alexander's forehead wrinkled, then a smile overcame his face as if he were relieved to finally share a piece of him he had to keep private from the world.

I unlaced my boots and held on to the attic door as Alexander helped me yank them off. He held my hand as I stepped into his coffin. The mattress was soft against my socks. I lay back, and pulled the cozy black duvet over me.

The candelabra gently lit the room and shadows danced around like tiny vampire bats. I smelled the sweet scent of Drakar on the pillow.

The casket was small and claustrophobic. The sides of the coffin entombed me. I felt like one of the undead.

"This is so cool!" I shrieked.

I smiled up at my boyfriend as he gazed down at me with pride.

"I'm ready."

"I don't think—"

"But I have to . . . I need to know what it's like."

A small handle had been nailed inside the lid with a dangling chain.

I reached up and grabbed the chain.

I took a deep breath. I gently pulled the chain toward me. The heavy lid began to lower slowly. Alexander's smiling face began to disappear from view. Then his shoulders, his AFI T-shirt. Finally all I saw was his handcuff belt buckle. Light in the coffin gradually turned to thick black darkness until I couldn't even see the chain I was pulling; then my own hand disappeared.

I felt as if I were being buried alive.

The coffin lid lifted open and a blast of light hit me.

"Alexander—" I could hear a faint voice call from the other room.

I squinted and tried to adjust to the candle-light as I sat up.

Alexander held out his hand and pulled me out.

"But I didn't get to—," I began, like a disappointed child.

"We've got to go—"

"Alexander," Jameson called as he rapped against the bedroom door. "I'm going to retire for the evening and I'd like to say good night to Miss Raven," the butler said.

Alexander grabbed my shoes, blew out the candles, and locked the closet.

"We'll be right there," Alexander called back as I pulled on my boots and laced them.

If Jameson had arrived a few minutes later, I would have known what it was like to retire for eternity.

That night, as I rested in my own bed—a spacious double bed, with no walls or lids—I wondered what it would have been like to have lain in Alexander's closed coffin. Total darkness, without so much as a faint streetlight shining in.

I imagined how hard it must have been for Alexander to let someone, anyone—even me— into his darkened world behind the secret attic door. I smiled, knowing what I must mean to him to be the one he shared it with.

As I closed my eyes, I imagined my true love spending his sunlit hours alone in his coffin, inside the confines of a hidden closet, buried away from any sources of life—the sounds of birds, rainfall, or people. The world that Alexander thought was so cold, dark, and lonely was just that. My heart broke and began to shatter into a million tiny pieces. Tears began to well up in my eyes, thinking while I was at school, surrounded by students and teachers, that the love of my life was locked away, alone in the dark. There was no one to touch, say sweet dreams to, kiss or squeeze. I wondered if the world I'd been romanticizing for so long—his world—as Alexander had often told me, wasn't so romantic after all.

The town of Dullsville returned to normal. Students at Dullsville High gossiped about the Graveyard Gala and the sickly siblings from Romania—"Were they really ghosts, vampires, or just goths like Raven?" There were no more sightings of Dullsville's motley twins at soccer games, Hatsy's Diner, or graveyards. School talk quickly turned to upcoming exams and proms.

Trevor, with his renewed popularity, was back to scoring on and off the soccer field. My stomach knotted, knowing he was even more popular than he had been before.

However, I did notice a slight change in my nemesis's behavior toward me. He didn't invite me to parties, drive me to school, or offer to carry my books, but I'd occasionally catch him staring at me. Once he signaled for Becky and me to cut ahead of him in the lunch line. When I dropped my English folder in the hallway, I was amazed when he said, "You dropped your notebook, Raven," instead of referring to me as "Monster Girl."

I was most surprised, though, when he cornered me at the drinking fountain one day and said, "I wonder what would have happened if it had been my family who moved into the Mansion instead of the Sterlings."

"Then Alexander would be talking to me right now instead of you," I said, and walked away.

I couldn't resist egging on my flirty nemesis.

I guess the soccer snob had gotten a taste of his own medicine—he knew what it was like not to be accepted. I'd let him soak it in a little longer.

Becky and I made a point of hanging out more—including a weekly after-school "girls only" shake snack at Hatsy's—while she and Matt continued dating.

The spring sun baked my pale skin and I was only comforted when the sun set and I could see Alexander again. During the evenings, Alexander and I snuck back into Dullsville's cemetery with garbage bags and picked up cans and bottles until we were exhausted. We discovered the coffins and nails and other gothic memorabilia were mysteriously removed from Henry's treehouse, presumably by Jagger as he and Luna fled Dullsville.

The following weekend Henry and his parents showed their appreciation for taking care of Henry. They planned a small backyard barbecue party for the Madison family and asked us to invite a few of our friends.

The backyard smelled of grilled hot dogs and

hamburgers, fresh baked buns, and all the dill pickles one could eat. The sky was clear, showcasing a million twinkling stars overhead. Henry and Billy Boy were attempting dives in the heated pool. Henry's mother was giving my mom a grand tour of their five-bedroom house. His father and my dad were practicing golf swings in the backyard. Nina, the housekeeper, was serving refreshments to Ruby and Jameson at a picnic table. The butler seemed grateful to have someone else wait on him for a change. Matt and Becky were eating s'mores and hanging by the flower garden.

Alexander and I sat together on a backyard swing. "This is like a dream come true," Alexander said as we gently swung back and forth. "We can finally just focus on us now. Continue the traditional 'Boy meets girl, girl falls for boy, boy turns out to be a vampire' story."

I laughed, and Alexander squeezed my hand. I could tell he was as relieved as I was to finally have Jagger and Luna gone from Dullsville.

"I'm going to miss my life as a vampire," I confessed softly. "I was really getting used to it. Hiding from the daylight, finding adventure in the moonlight. Hanging out with a vampiress. I have to admit that there is a tiny part of me that is going to miss Luna, maybe because she has a life I'd always dreamed of, or maybe because she accepted me. And there's a slight part of me that will think fondly of Jagger—not his vengeful side, but his passion for who he is—a vampire."

"It's okay to have mixed feelings for them," Alexander assured me. "They were unlike anyone you'd ever known before. That's how I feel about you."

"I felt like I had found a group where I finally fit in—mortal or not."

"That's how I feel when I'm with you. We really do belong together," Alexander said, his lonely eyes a little less lonely. "No matter where we are."

Then I remembered how isolated I felt when we were apart. Even though his darkened world may not have been as romantic as I'd imagined, how bad could it be if we were in it, together?

"Maybe sometime soon we can make my dream more permanent . . . ," I suggested. It was fun to have vampires believe I was one of them. Now I just have to convince a third. But then I wondered if Jagger was right when he said I was more like a vampire than Alexander was. If I were turned into a vampire, would I be the kind of vampire Alexander was—or the kind that Jagger and Luna were?

I looked at Alexander, waiting for his response.

Billy Boy climbed out of the pool. He ran over to me and shook his wet hair at me like a soaked dog.

"Get off, you creep!" I shouted, covering myself from the spray.

My brother laughed, and I noticed even Alexander chuckling as he wiped water off his pale arm. Billy Boy ran over to the lounge chair where his stuff lay before I could wring his neck.

"Maybe we can sleep out in the treehouse now that your parents are back," Billy Boy said to Henry as he grabbed his towel.

"Yeah," he said, climbing out of the pool. "I have to get it cleaned up before that dude comes over to look at it."

"Is someone planning to buy your treehouse?" I teased.

"Just doing a report on it," Billy Boy said

proudly. "Henry and I overheard this dude at the library asking the librarian for info on area treehouses. Naturally Henry has the coolest one, so I had to tell him about it."

"Well, you should be careful inviting strangers over," I warned, sounding like my mother.

"He's not dangerous," Billy said. "He's only eleven and skinnier than I am."

"But he is kind of strange," Henry admitted.

Billy Boy laughed as he toweled off his hair. "He is major strange—looks like he should be your brother instead of me," Billy Boy teased. "Pale skin, pierced ears, black fingernails."

I stopped the swing. "Does this kid have a name?"

Billy Boy nodded.

"What is it?" I demanded in his face.

"It'll cost you," he said.

"It will cost you more if you don't tell me," I said, taking his towel, threatening to snap it at his feet.

"Fine," he said through gritted teeth. "It's Valentine." He yanked back his towel. "His name is Valentine Maxwell."

Valentine? That was the name of Luna's younger brother. An eleven-year-old vampire.

I looked at Alexander, who gave me a knowing glance.

I froze. My blood raced. My heart stopped.

Oh. My. Goth. It was one thing to have met a nefarious vengeful teen vampire, then to encounter the wrath of his newly turned twin sister, and have them turn my world upside down. It was quite another to have a preteen vampire now lurking and hanging out in the same library and treehouse as my younger sibling.

I couldn't even fathom an eleven-year-old vampire—his motives, what he hungered for, what powers he might possess.

If Jagger and Luna had disappeared on the night of the Graveyard Gala, what was their younger vampire brother, Valentine, doing in Dullsville?

I knew one thing—I'd have to find out.

Acknowledgments

W ith my utmost gratitude I would like to thank the following fabulous people:

Katherine Tegen, my phenomenal editor, for making the *Vampire Kisses* series possible. Your expertise, friendship, humor, and always insightful direction have enhanced my life and my work. Thanks for making my dreams come true!

Ellen Levine, my extraordinary agent, for your amazing advice and talent and for being an inspiration in guiding my career.

Julie Lansky at HarperCollins, for your wonderful suggestions, help, and friendship.

231

My brother, Mark Schreiber, for being my mentor and for helping me become the writer I am today.

My brother, Ben Schreiber, for your endless enthusiasm and support.

And Eddie Lerer, for being my Alexander and taking me out of Dullsville.

Read on for a preview of the fourth book
in the chilling Vampire Kisses series:

Dance with a Vampire

I awoke from a deadly slumber entombed in
Alexander's coffin.

Since arriving at the Mansion shortly before
Sunday morning's sunrise, I'd been lying next to
my vampire boyfriend, Alexander Sterling, as he
slept the weekend sunlit hours away, hidden in
the closet of his attic room.

This was a dream come true. My first real
taste—or in this case, bite—of the vampire
lifestyle.

We nestled in my true love's bed—a claustrophobic black wooden casket. I was as blind as any
bat; we could have been buried in the deepest

recesses of a long-forgotten cemetery. Encased in our compacted quarters, I could easily touch the closed lid above me and brush my elbow against the side wall. The sweet scents of pine and cedar floated around me like incense. I couldn't see anything, not even my own black-fingernailed hand. No sounds were audible from outside the coffin. Not a siren, a bird, or the howling wind. I even lost track of time. I felt like we were the only two people in the world—that nothing existed outside these confining coffin walls.

Blanketed by darkness and a soft-as-a-spider's-web goose-feathered duvet, I was enveloped in Alexander's arctic white arms, my head gently resting against his chest. I felt his warm breath against my cheek. I imagined his deadly pale lids covering his chocolate brown eyes. I playfully fingered his velvet lips and brushed my fingertips over his perfect teeth until I felt one as sharp as a knife.

I tasted my finger for blood. Unfortunately, there was none.

I was so close to being part of Alexander's world—forever.

Or was I?

Though it was Sunday and I was exhausted from having spent the past few weeks protecting my nemesis, Trevor Mitchell, from the fangs of twin vampires, Jagger and Luna Maxwell, I was restless. I couldn't change my sleeping pattern from night to day.

Cuddling close to Alexander and sharing his world, I wanted nothing more than to spend our time kissing, playing, and talking.

But as he slept tranquilly, I could only think of one thing: A preteen vampire had descended upon Dullsville. And his name was Valentine.

The younger brother of the nefarious Nosferatu twins had arisen from his own petite coffin a few days before from somewhere in the vampire world and had been spotted in Dullsville by my brother and his nerd-mate, Henry.

I could only presume what Valentine looked like based on my brother's description: pale skin, pierced ears, black fingernails. I imagined a smaller version of Jagger—cryptic, gaunt, ghastly. How cruel it was that Jagger's sibling was just like him, and mine the polar opposite of me. If only I had been blessed with a ghoulish little brother. We'd have spent our childhood chasing ghosts in Dullsville's cemetery, searching Oakley Woods for creepy spiders, and playing hide-and-shriek in our basement. Instead, I grew up with a brother who'd prefer to dissect square roots alone rather than dissect gummi worms together.

I wondered why Valentine suddenly showed up in the conservative town of Dullsville, far away from his Romanian homeland. Now that Alexander and I were free from the older Maxwell siblings, I'd set forth on a new mission—finding out the eleven-year-old Valentine's whereabouts and motives and keeping him from Billy Boy before it was too late. But during the sunlight hours, my brother and Dullsville were in no danger, so my mind strayed back to the only vampire I felt secure with.

As Alexander and I lay in the dark, entombed and entwined, I stroked his silky black hair.

There was no place for me in the daylight without him. I had accepted the dangers Alexander had so warned me about, but I couldn't spend an eternity in the scorching sun minus my true love. Didn't Alexander know how easily I could adapt to his world, sleeping together in our cozy casket, flying together in the night sky, living in the dusty old Mansion? I wondered what type of vampire I'd be: A gentle dreamer like Alexander or a bloodthirsty menace like Jagger? Either way, since Jagger and Luna had departed from Dullsville, Alexander and I finally had a chance to share our mortal and immortal worlds. However, there could be an obstacle in my way, now that Valentine was in town.

Alexander stirred. He, too, couldn't sleep.

"You're awake," he whispered sweetly. "I'm sure it must be hard for you to adjust your sleep schedule."

I didn't want to admit that I couldn't be the perfect vampiress.

"I can't rest with you so close to me. I feel more alive than ever," I said.

My fingers felt around his smooth face and found his soft lips. I leaned in to kiss him, but my nose accidentally bumped into his.

"I'm sorry," I said with a giggle.

"One of the drawbacks of dating a mortal," he teased, a smile in his voice. "But it's worth it."

"What do you mean?"

Instead of answering, he lightly touched my cheek, sending tingles through my body.

Then he pressed his lips to mine and raced his fingers down my spine. I thought I was going to die. My hair flopped in my face, and he did something I couldn't fathom doing in the dark.

He gently brushed it away.

I gasped.

"How did you know my hair was hanging in my eyes?"

Alexander didn't answer.

"You can see!" I said blindly. "You can see me."

"I'm very lucky," he finally admitted. "You happen to be quite beautiful."

There were so many mysteries to Alexander, I wondered how many more would be revealed to me—and how I could unlock them.

I buried my head in his chest as he gently caressed my back.

"The sun has set," he said matter-of-factly.

"Already? How can you tell?" I asked. "You can see that, too?"

But he didn't answer.

I could hear Alexander lift the coffin lid. He grabbed my hand and I reluctantly rose, standing in total darkness.

Alexander scooped me up in his arms and carried me out of the casket like Dracula holding his mortal bride. He gently lowered me and I hung close to him, unaware of our exact location. The doorknob squeaked and the closet door creaked open. I squinted as my eyes tried to adjust to the beam of moonlight that pierced the room.

We pulled on our combat boots as I sat on his beat-up comfy chair and Alexander knelt on the uneven hardwood floor.

"So, will you teach me to fly?" I asked, half teasing.

"Valentine is not the kind of boy Billy should be hanging out with. We must get to your brother before Valentine does."

With that, Alexander locked the closet door, grabbed my hand, and, for now, closed the portal to the Underworld.

Watch out, Dullsville....
Alexander's dangerous cousin has come for a visit.

More juicy stories about Raven and Alexander!

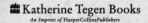

www.harperteen.com